James C Dibdin

The Cleekim Inn

A tale of smuggling in the '45

James C Dibdin

The Cleekim Inn
A tale of smuggling in the '45

ISBN/EAN: 9783337071349

Printed in Europe, USA, Canada, Australia, Japan

Cover: Foto ©Andreas Hilbeck / pixelio.de

More available books at **www.hansebooks.com**

THE
CLEEKIM INN

THE
CLEEKIM INN

A Tale of Smuggling in the '45

By

JAMES C. DIBDIN

WESTMINSTER

ARCHIBALD CONSTABLE

AND CO 1896

Edinburgh : T. and A. Constable, Printers to Her Majesty

FOR REASONS

KNOWN TO ONLY TWO

THIS VOLUME

IS DEDICATED TO

MY WIFE

INTRODUCTION.

THERE are people who will tell you, that having visited a particular place for the first time in their lives, they are surprised at its seeming familiarity to their sense of sight. A scene, a corner of a field, a hillside or a house front, is to them as an old friend suddenly re-introduced.

It is the same with faces. You meet a person for the first time in your life, yet could swear to having been acquainted with him or her before; not only with the face, but more particularly with the personality.

Those who look for an explanation no deeper than the surface will banish astonishment and end dispute by saying, "You must have dreamt of it." Truly, but wherefore? He that says the full explanation of an animal's appetite is that he is hungry gives you only a fractional portion of the full reason. In this

A

excellently ordered world there is a reason for everything, although frequently it does not lie on the surface. For Dreaming there may be many reasons. Some contend that the soul leaves the body entirely and mingles with other disembodied spirit-companions in the ethereal regions between this and the moon. Perhaps it does. Digestion (or the lack of it) is, to others, responsible for all; but, although lobster salad and champagne may conjure up most extraordinary nightmares, it is hard to comprehend how it can exhibit before the camera of the mind pictures of scenes hundreds of miles away and never previously beheld.

So much, however, it is conceivable that some of the little understood laws of heredity can do, although it is not always easy or possible to follow the chain of events from the first impulse being given, to the time when you are startled by the familiar appearance of person, place, or thing upon which, you can prove, your eyes have never before looked.

The writer experienced this peculiar feeling when he first had the delight of seeing Miss Terry act. It was at Liverpool some twelve or fifteen years ago. Not only her face, but her voice and actions, nay, the workings of her very soul, seemed familiar, as if at some past time she and he had been friends in thought and sympathy. But the time that has elapsed has brought no solution of the problem.

It was different with a friend, who, on visiting for the first time in his life a certain spot in the Border Country, at once recognised it as the scene of many of his dreams for years and years before.

For long after no explanation was forth-coming; and then it startled him when it was. The scene lay where four cross-roads met, and he discovered that his grandfather had been a smuggler, and had been killed upon that very spot in a scrimmage with the Custom House Officers, *and was buried where he fell!*

It may be asked, what connection has this with the following tale? To which may be given the reply : "Much!" It suggested it.

CHAPTER I.

IT was in the autumn of the year 1745, on a cold, wet, misty afternoon, that the door of the Cleekim Inn was opened from within by a stout, ill clad, worse washed, but not unattractive looking female of perhaps forty years of age, who, walking to the western corner of the building, gazed long and anxiously up the steep road that "climbed" the hill to the south. There was nothing moving save the swaying firs and the dribbling streams that, without any reverence for the venerable Roman paving which they disturbed, cut courses for themselves, until they combined with a tributary burn flowing into the Teviot. Not a sound could be heard save the trickle-trickle of rain-drops from every leaf, and afar off the musical gurgle of the swollen river.

Satisfied apparently, after a protracted gaze, of what one glance might have revealed, she retraced her steps to the door of the inn, and shouted "ben" in a loud voice: "The packs are no in sicht, and I'se warrant they'll no get free frae Jeddart th' nicht." To which a female voice from within replied, "Gud a' mercy, if Wull Scott's wi' them, they'll no be far awa'."

Another expedition to the corner resulted in an exclamation, "There they are noo": and, sure enough there appeared, upon the ridge against the cold grey sky beyond, certain gaunt and, more or less, shapeless moving shadows, which, diving one by one into the nearer but darker middle distance of the road and into the shadow of the pines, were lost to sight for the moment.

Presently half a score of "gentlemen" surrounded the door of the inn with, in addition to their own manly presences, three times the number of horses, each one of which was heavily laden with casks, chests, and cunningly made up bundles and parcels. There was some resemblance about the cavalcade to a caravan crossing the desert which, having hit upon a convenient oasis, halts for rest and refreshment. The chief difference in the present case was,

that instead of the animals being attended
to first, man, the lord of creation, raised his
voice, loudly demanding refreshment, while
his four-footed companions made shift to find
for themselves some sustenance in the long
grass that grew by the roadside. Great hurrying and shuffling were to be heard now within
the house, while the owners of gruff-sounding
voices were roaring to each other, as well as
to the possessors of the two shriller pipes
whose acquaintance we have already made.
In a few minutes two of the men emerged
from the house; one, a tall bony stripling,
was instructed by his senior to "keep his
eyes skinned," and see that the beasts did
not stray, and that no strangers approached,
without due warning being given to the
company within.

The elder man re-entered the tavern, where, in
the kitchen, his companions were seated. Some
of them were already quaffing sweet ale from
huge tankards, while one or two, despising
the brew of their own land, sipped cautiously
the still almost boiling rum and water, which
had been placed before them.

Wilder and louder grew the language of

the men, while the high priestess of these bacchanals served, with evident delight, repeated supplies of liquor. The conversation, from being general and not over-burdened with decency, especially when addressed to the middle-aged occupants of the inn, soon became centred on the then all-engrossing theme: Prince Charlie's march and successful entry into Edinburgh. From John o' Groat's to Carlisle little else was spoken about, and little else thought about, and if in the more sedate portions of the country the excitement rose to almost fever-pitch, what did it not do in the very heart of the borders, where blood had always run swifter and hearts beat quicker than elsewhere.

There were few "Border bloods" at that time who did not hail the advancing army with delight, while with such as the occupants of the inn, at the moment we have arrived at, whose way of life lay not in beaten tracks, the vista that was opened out to the imagination of chances of booty and plunder served to inflame their blood to an extent scarcely conceivable in these piping times of peace.

Without wasting words, let the reader understand that the men of the gang, which has been introduced to him, were smugglers, whose headquarters were in Jedburgh, a town then, and for years afterwards, of supreme notoriety for its contraband trade. The present expedition had started *en route* for Edinburgh that very afternoon, and, as was not unusual in such cases, had come to a sudden and protracted halt, owing to the seductive potency of the Cleekim ale. Will. Scott, who was the leader of the gang, was a young, resolute, and broad-shouldered man of thirty or thereby, who, despite his comparatively few years, had already acquired much reputation as being a daring and successful runner of contraband goods. The old Border spirit was keenly alive in him, and the love of adventure and the charm of the rough life, with its dangers and coarse material pleasures, were more to him than any thoughts of gain.

Repeatedly had he made successful sallies through the lines of the Custom House officers, and triumphantly deposited his charges of smuggled goods in the hands of the merchant to whom they had been consigned. Although not altogether actuated in his business by any sordid love of gain, there can be no question that the substantial reward placed in his hand, upon his arrival in the capital, was fully appreciated, if for no other reason than the power it gave him of enjoying, for a brief three or four weeks, an amount of luxurious and costly idleness among all the fascinations of the town, that could not be procured in the country.

Upon his present journey, however, something much more enticing than mere temporary pleasures attracted him towards his goal. Love of adventure was his strongest passion, and could there be a better chance than the present to indulge it freely, and with every chance of great reward? He and his companions, in common with the bulk of the population of the country districts in Scotland, possessed but mean ideas of the power of England once it should be called into play. To their imagination the advance of the Highlanders must prove irresistible, and the golden gates of London would be opened by a soft and enervated populace without a struggle. What a glorious future for the Jacobites then! Prince Charles not only would enjoy his own again; but he would scatter his rewards to his faithful followers, at the expense of the Hanoverians.

To be first in the risk would be to come fore-
most in sharing the spoils which the restored
King would give with a lavish hand. So, at
any rate, thought those who allowed impulse
and ambition to get the better of their soberer
judgments. The inhabitants of the towns knew
better and wisely kept quiet; judging such
policy safest and remembering that silence is
always likened to gold, but speech frequently to a
vastly inferior metal. Perhaps a glimmering of
a nobler and more exalted spirit may have
possessed Will. Scott, impelling him to use
his energies for more legitimate pursuits than
smuggling. Warfare was a game in which kings
generally played a principal part, and opened up
unbounded chances of elevation and promotion.
Smuggling never could do more for its servants
than elevate them to the height of a gallows
tree ! So with one and all, " To the wars " was
the word that evening in the Cleekim Inn.
Every member of the gang was a stout
Jacobite, and great were the resolves and large the
promises made ; these ever grew greater as the
ale became less, until, having reached a meridian
in their course, sleep and drunken stupor must
soon have supervened, and the morning's light

would scarcely have found the evening's sentiments endorsed with acclaim. Suddenly the
noise of boastful brawling was changed into
hurried shoutings of preparations for departure
in the instant, for the youth, who had remained
sentry without, came in with terrified face to say
that "the beacons were on fire from the far off
Eildons to the Cheviots."

In a moment the gang rushed pell mell to
their horses, which they had no difficulty in
seeing and mounting, for although the sun had
long been sunk into the west, the misty air
was filled with a dull red glare, which lent
its powerful aid in making the picture of these
roughly clad and heavily armed men a weird
and uncanny sight.

As they rushed about, howling and swearing
at the top of their voices, the shrill voice of the
landlady rose above the din and clatter of the
storm, like the shriek of an eagle when it feels
its prey slipping from its grasp.

"Pay me ma lawin', ye wretches! Pay me
ma lawin'! Wull Scott! Wull Scott! pay me,
ye blackguard; or it'll be the worse for ye"!

"To hell wi' you an' yer lawin'! ye
jade! D'ye no see the fires? There's war,

an' oor King needs oor help. We'll pay ye
when we come back."

"An' when'll that be, think ye? Leave the
King to dae as he likes best hissel', an' stick
to yer trade."

"We'll come back an' pay ye, ne'er fear!"
roared one of the men. "We'll be back afore
the year's out, onyway."

"We'll a' come back this day twalmonth
an' pay ye, ye scullion," cried another.

"An' see ye hae oor dinner het an' smokin'!" added Will. Scott.

"Syne ye dae come back," shrieked the dame,
fearful of offending such slippery customers too
far, "Syne ye dae come back, I'll hae yer dinner
het, Wull Scott, an' see ye bring gowd to pay
the reckoning an' interest."

"We'll a' be back, never fear!" and as
several voices called out, "It's a tryst!" the
leader vaulted nimbly into his saddle.

In a moment the whole cavalcade was in
motion and, in another, would have been lost
to sight in the mist. One of the beacon fires
that was nearest sent forth at that moment a
brighter blaze of light. It dyed the shift-
ing mist around to a blood-red glow when,

there suddenly appeared, facing the horsemen, as if it had sprung out of the earth or been evolved from the watery vapour, a wild unearthly apparition, a description of which, however minute or graphic, would fall far short in conveying any adequate idea of the actual thing appearing, as it did under such circumstances. Superstitious as the smugglers were at all times, this weird apparition was well calculated to intensify the terrible and supernatural impressions that had already filled the breasts, not only of the small party of horsemen, but also of the lady of the inn, as she was in the act of making one last appeal to Will. Scott for her " lawin'."

The horses shared the sudden fright of their masters; some reared and plunged, while others stood trembling as if paralysed.

The apparition flourished a stick in its hand, and made frantic gestures to the band to go back the way it had come, while it (or " she "—it makes little difference which) shrieked aloud :— " Tryst ye trysts in hell if ye gang that gate, Wull Scott. Back, back tae Jeddart, I say, and turn not."

Not content with this menacing exordium, the beldam stretched forth her hands, and catching Will Scott's bridle, contrived by the exertion of what seemed superhuman strength to drag horse and man completely round.

So taken by surprise was he, that, for a moment, not a finger did he lift to free himself and his horse from her clutch; but prompt action was too much the man's nature for him to forget himself long, and, with a whisk of his riding whip and a pull at the rein, he righted himself quickly.

The whip had inflicted a cruel cut across the creature's face, and blood flowed freely over her eyes, as, with language of a character not meet to be set down, she hurled curses of all kinds at Will. Scott. " Gang," at last she yelled after him, as putting spurs to his horse he rode into the mist; " Gang, gang tae yer fate, ye ill-faured scoondrel ! Gang ! an' mind yer tryst ! "

The horsemen had gone out of sight, and the thud of the hoofs had died away. The hag remained without moving, but continued her curses in a voice that gradually sunk into an unintelligible mutter. As for the landlady, she still stood on the spot as if petrified, till the hag, turning her head towards her, broke the spell.

"G'awa, auld wumman; or if yer tired an' hard up, there's drink an' welcome, but dinna bide an' bring misfortune to ma door."

"D'ye see yon man?" mused the old crone, without paying any heed to what had been said to her. "D'ye see yon man? Na! ye canna, for the mist that's atween him an' you. Nae mair can ye see through the mist o' the future, ma lassie! but, I can, I can."

"What can ye see?" gasped the other, impelled by a curiosity she could not restrain.

"What can I see? What can I no see? I can see. Ay! I can see the tartan plaids a' dyed wi' bluid, as red's that licht. I can hear the groans o' the deein' like the soughin' o' th' wind in the trees. Ah!" and she gave a scream that sent a cold shiver up her hearer's back. "There is bluid here, here! on this vera stane, an' ma lassie, I'll tak yer drink, for I've far tae gang.

> "An a' my sang
> Is bluid, bluid, bluid."

In abject fear, and with trembling hand, the landlady served her with a tumbler of raw spirit, which the hag tossed off as if it had been small beer, and without a word of farewell or thanks, turned and departed into the mist, from which a few seconds afterwards there came a voice of ill omen.

> " Will Scott will meet his quean
> In Edinburgh toun,
> It's there the lad is gane
> To buy for her a goun,
> And he will keep his tryst
> As safe as e'er betide—"

but the remainder was lost in the distance, and Helen Kenway, for such was the name of the landlady, retired hurriedly into her house, the door of which she shut and barred with a stout oaken beam that fitted into two deep holes in the wall, thus forming an almost impregnable barricade.

B

CHAPTER II.

ALL that night the cavalcade continued its journey at a rapid pace. When the morning of another day awoke, it was to behold Will. Scott's band cantering briskly along the level stretch of sward by the side of the Leader Water, a mile or so above the ancient town of Earlston. The smugglers had made good progress, the darkness and mist being small hindrance to them, who knew the road so well. The ford over the Tweed, a little above Leader Foot, was considerably flooded, and, for horses less sure of foot or riders less certain of their ground, might have proved dangerous; but to these men neither the dangers of flood nor of gaugers were of much consideration beyond the necessity for caution and prompt action when necessary.

A thick patch of forest near by Huntshaw Hill was selected by the party as a halting ground. Fires were made and a coarse meal of

bannocks and cheese, washed down with draughts
of rum, was swallowed with little grace or ceremony, after which a watch was set, and the
chorus of snores that immediately followed
proved how fatigued every one was with the
labours of the night.

The sun mounted above the " Black Hill," and
as it crossed the meridian dispelled the remnants
of the previous night's mist. But it was not
until the orb of light had got well home to the
west, that one by one the smugglers wakened,
and about an hour before sunset were again
mounted and on their northward journey.

Avoiding all chance meetings with rustics as
much as possible, they came to the brow of the
hill, from which, in the quickly departing daylight, they could see Carfrae Mill with its cluster
of surrounding huts, which included an inn,
famous yet for its welcome refreshment to
cyclists who have braved the northern steeps
and descended the southern slope of Soutra Hill.

In the days of which we write it served a
double purpose : first, as a convenient resting-
place for the Custom House officers, who were
known frequently to hover somewhere upon this
particular part of the road, on the look out for

smugglers, who, for their part, if they thought the coast was clear, generally halted to rest and refresh themselves before mounting the hill. **Will.** Scott was particularly anxious on this occasion to spend an hour or two in this harbour, as he had an appointment with the landlady, whose husband he knew would be from home; but caution necessitated the despatch in the first place of a spy to see what was going on. Entering one of the neighbouring huts, this individual ascertained from the friendly inhabitants that the inn was presently occupied by a large party of gaugers, who had arrived from the north in evident haste not an hour before.

This information being reported, it was deemed important to proceed at once on the journey, leaving their natural enemies behind, with the prospect of enjoying a clear road ahead. Unwilling as Scott was to carry out this plan of action, necessity knows no law, and the risk of waiting where he was was too great.

In good time the great level stretch of moss on the summit of Soutra Hill was reached, and there the horses broke into a quicker pace; man and beast seemed anxious to gain the shelter of the hospitable inn that stood by the side of the mountain road, almost the only house within sight, and which, like that at Carfrae Mill, was generally occupied by smugglers or their foes, the representatives of the Government.

On this occasion caution was not considered necessary. The large gathering of the hateful class at the foot of the hill forbade the chance of any being posted in the Soutra Inn as well, and so the cavalcade rode on without caution, and ensconced themselves with little ceremony.

At the present day, scarcely a stone stands on another to mark what was once the prosperous and gay village of Soutra, famous in its time as a place of sanctuary, and dedicated, by those who found it convenient to breathe freedom from danger in the mountain air it afforded, to feasting and revelry. Long ere Will. Scott first crossed the Lammermoor Hills, the glories of the erst-while village had departed. The reforming clergy had long before stripped it of its revenues, its privileges had been torn from it, and only the solitary public house remained as a monument pointing out the uncertainty of all things human. Nations, towns, villages, people, all must bow to the inevitable changes that are brought about by time; like this village of Soutra, once so gay, now desolate, they must at length face decay and dissolution.

But our smuggling friends had neither inclination nor time for such reflections, and were content to practise what has at one time been stated to be the height and at another the lowest depth of all philosophy :—"Eat, drink, and be merry; for no man can command the morrow."

In which laudable undertakings, on this occasion, they were aided with almost suspicious eagerness by the landlady. No suspicions, however, entered their heads, and so careless had the occupants of the inn become, in the knowledge that their enemies were miles away, at the foot of the hill, that no guard had been set as yet; and it was nearing midnight. At this hour, the door of the inn was opened from without and a stranger entered. He was a tall, well built man, of about forty years of age, with dark red hair, and jet black eyes; while a large nose, and prominent chin, marked him as courageous, self-reliant, and prompt in action.

With a pleasant "Good e'en!" to the company, he turned to the landlady, and called for a bottle of wine.

" 'Deed!" she cried, bustling up to her new

customer with what seemed anything but
hospitable intentions, "'Deed! ye'll wine nae
wines this gate! ye're owre late! sae just tak'
the road ye've come! shae leather's cheap!"

"My good woman!" remonstrated the
stranger, seating himself at the same time near
the small hole in the wall that served for a
window; "my good woman, you are very un-
reasonable! I am sure my demand is quite
legitimate. I—"

But he was interrupted by her whom he
addressed: "Don't 'good woman' me, ma man!
My name's M'Tavish, an' gin ye no—" But
what promised to become a heated quarrel (on
one side, at all events) was stopped by the
sound of a clenched fist brought down with
the weight of a sledge hammer on the rough
table, making the glasses and plates jump
again; and a voice, as of thunder, uttering the
single word, " Silence !"

The behests of Jove himself were never
carried out with such alacrity as was this. It
was Will. Scott who had spoken, and, turning
in his chair to where the stranger sat, he addressed him: "This inn is occupied; if ye
want tae drink, you dae sae at ma expense, an'

then ye flit. Quick! gie it a name, an' it 'll be brocht."

"Excuse me," was the reply, "I do not drink with strangers," saying which, he rose and made for the door; but one of Scott's men, on a sign from his chief, was too quick, and stood between him and freedom; but it was only for a moment. In less time than it takes to read six words of this account, the smuggler was lying on his face, dead, with a bullet in his brain, and the stranger was outside the door of the inn. Several shots were sent after him, and then followed a wild chase to the door. What happened there no powers of description can picture. A trap had been laid by the Custom House officers, and most cleverly and successfully was it carried out.

As usual, a woman was at the bottom of the mischief. Will Scott was as noted for his gallantry to the ladies as he was for his bravery and success in his dangerous calling; and the landladies of the different inns he frequented upon his journeys, came in for a good deal of his attentions. Now; it is an established rule of human nature, that in proportion as a man is free in bestowing his attentions on the fair sex, so does the latter become jealous of these attentions being divided. That is to say, women are oftenest most jealous of, and fondest of the most worthless men. Even among the educated and refined it is so, although to a less degree than with those whose animal passions are unrestrained by culture and education. Will. Scott, like so many of his sex before and since, imagined that in knowing how to please women, he held as well the key to understanding their natures! Idle belief! born of self-sufficiency, and certain to be destroyed at the moment just when one's plans appear on the point of a successful consummation. In paying attentions to these women, Scott rightly judged that there was little chance of their telling one another particulars of their acquaintanceship with him ; but he did not reckon on that subtle art by which women (especially such as are of a jealous nature) learn, seemingly by intuition, when those they love forfeit their esteem and prove undeserving of their continued affection.

The lady of the Soutra Inn had a long-standing and deeply-rooted grudge against the landlady of the Carfrae Mill Inn. The latter was younger and better looking (sufficient cause for

jealousy always), and since her arrival at
Carfrae Mill, some two years before, had completely taken Scott's heart captive. Without
having a scrap of actual evidence, this fact had
been divined by Mrs M'Tavish ; and, her un-
reasoning jealousy being based upon a passion
of the lowest and most degraded sort, she
naturally sought for revenge of the most malig-
nant nature.

This is how she managed to obtain it. A
few days before the events already narrated
took place, a party of Custom officers from
Dalkeith arrived at her inn. It was under
the direction of no less a person than he of the
red hair and black eyes we have left for a few
moments, and who, by a winning manner and
pleasant address, not only charmed the lonely
widow M'Tavish, but contrived to draw from
her the grand secret of her jealousy of Will.
Scott and the young wife of Carfrae Mill. This
he used as a key to unlock all the rest, and
by planning the march to Carfrae Mill, when
his scouts informed him the gang of smugglers
was nearing there, he rightly calculated on
putting the latter off the scent. To retrace
their steps, follow their intended prey up to

Soutra, and surprise them while they were
enjoying their liquor in fancied security, was
the next move; but the way in which it was
carried out was in the best style of general-
ship. His entering the inn, alone, was carefully arranged. First of all, he wished to know
accurately how many, and who, composed the
gang; secondly, he knew the danger that would
attend entering the house with a hostile intent. Pistols in the hands of desperate men
are dangerous weapons to encounter at short
range. So his original design had been (after
a scene with the landlady, which, with the rest,
was planned and paid for, her reward being
twenty guineas) to fire his pistol into the room
as he left at the door, knowing well if he did so
that the smugglers would return his fire, and
so empty their pistols, and most likely sally out
after him. He was a brave man, but not, as
might be thought, recklessly so, for he calculated
full well that he would be outside the door
before the pistol balls could reach him, and then
his men would be ready to pounce upon and
disarm the smugglers as they issued from the
door in his pursuit. Will. Scott's interruption was unexpected, but served as well as

anything else as an excuse to leave. The interposition of one of the gang between him and the door was even less calculated upon, and only the promptest action at that moment could have saved him.

The result was entirely successful. The smugglers, although reduced in numbers by one, still outnumbered the officers, but, on the other hand, they were taken at so great a disadvantage that, although they fought and struggled with savage fury, in a few minutes every one of them was captured.

Everything had contributed to this. The unexpected nature of the attack, their own eyes coming from the bright blaze of a pine log fire, could not penetrate the darkness, whereas the officers could see with perfect distinctness, their eyes having become accustomed to the want of light.

But in spite of all, one of the smugglers escaped. It was Will. Scott, who on the first impulse had likewise run to the door, but instantly checked himself, and knowing another way of escape through the inner kitchen, was soon safely outside, actually looking on at the struggle from a distance. He took in the whole situation at a glance, and although he felt prompted to rush forward and give battle, he could see that such a step would only lead to himself being taken with the rest, or killed without being able to effect any good. Instead, therefore, he stole quietly round to the stable and picked out what, as far as he could judge in the darkness, he thought the best horse, and mounting it made a dash for freedom.

It so happened he was compelled to pass within a few yards of the door, where still stood a couple of the victorious gaugers; they heard the clatter of the hoofs, and a couple of pistol balls whistled past his ears. To turn in his saddle and return the compliment took but a moment, and the dead smuggler still lying in the kitchen of the inn was avenged by that shot. A life had been taken for a life.

CHAPTER III.

NOT until he arrived at Craigmillar did Will. Scott draw rein, and then only when four or five ragged Highlanders darted out of a hut crying in a wild tone, and at the same time presenting their pieces, " Fourich, Fourich ! " (Stop, stop.)

"What d' ye want, ye dirty, lousy lookin' thieves ? " queried Scott, " d' ye no ken I'm for the Prince ? "

But he might as well have addressed the walls of the castle that towered above him, for the half-clad savages whom he faced understood as little Scots as he did Gaelic. A bright idea, however, struck him, and suiting the action to the thought, he felt in his pockets and extracted a few groats and smaller coins, which he flung to the Highlanders. The effect was entirely satisfactory, and he was allowed to pass.

Within half a mile he was again challenged, but ere this took place, the grey light of dawn had increased sufficiently to allow him to note the nature of the saddle upon which he rode. It was new and finely made, two convenient pouches held a brace of beautifully finished horse pistols, silver-mounted and loaded, while a small saddle bag, neatly concealed, on being opened, displayed to his astonished gaze a nest of guineas, certainly not less than two hundred in number.

He was not a man to remain long in either doubt or astonishment, so when challenged for the second time by the outposts of the Prince's army, he boldly and loudly demanded to be shown to head-quarters.

While the guard was debating in Gaelic what should be done with this stranger, an officer rode up, no other than Lochiel, who, ever polished in manner and gentle by nature, inquired in courteous terms what he could do for the new comer.

"I see," said the latter, "that ye 're a gentleman, and I dou't na an officer of the Prince's, so if ye tak me tac him I'll be michty weel pleased."

The countenance of Lochiel became suffused as this speech was in progress with a distinct smile; but when the smuggler or ex-smuggler, as he may now be termed, paused for a reply, it was with perfect gravity the Highlander replied, "If you will inform me of your name and desire, I shall make it my business to request an interview for you with His Highness the Prince."

"Ma name is Armstrong, of Laidlay Tower, and I hae come a' this gate to join the army o' the Prince."

"I congratulate you, sir, on your bravery and loyalty, and the Prince on having acquired so stout a soldier; I shall be much pleased, Mr Armstrong, provided it is agreeable to the Prince's wishes, that you should serve under myself."

"An' richt prood wad I be," replied Scott, who had enough discernment to see that he was in conversation with some one of high position in the army. This fact, and the knowledge of being actually on his way to an audience with the Prince, whom he believed would in a few months be King of England, and who, for the matter of that, might very easily have been had he been backed by proper troops instead of yelling savages—these reflections crowding together soon produced a feeling in Scott's mind altogether novel. It was undoubtedly a loftier one than had actuated the man during his entire career. The smuggler, thief, and murderer were forgotten, buried for ever; instead, there was something he believed to be a gentleman and soldier, on the eve of being introduced to his sovereign by a noble of the land !

Scott was neither the first nor the last of the race of scoundrels who had the makings of better things within him, had opportunity served to bring them out. The allurements held out by vice, Scott had long known. Not that he considered smuggling a vice. It was a business, or rather a profession; but not by any means so glorious a one as warfare. But the inducements to become a soldier had never been worthy consideration, beside the temptations which were held out by smuggling. The most he could have done, was to have joined as a common soldier and serve in the ranks; whereas as a smuggler, he was regarded as a leader, and his word was law. But here, under the frowning brow of Samson's Ribs, things took upon themselves an entirely new complexion.

More than one consideration had prompted Scott to give Lochiel a false name. He knew that the strange captain of the Custom House officers would leave no stone unturned to find and arrest him, although in joining the Prince's standard, he believed nearly all chance of being taken as an ex-smuggler was gone; at the same time, there was no harm in using due caution; besides, his own pride of nature, and perhaps of race, suggested he should enroll under the best possible auspices, especially now that he had got the means to live like a gentleman. Everything smiled upon him, and so he chose the name of the son of a Border laird, who was about his own age, and not unlike himself, he had been told, in appearance.

Arriving within the camp, Scott was taken by Lochiel to the portion occupied by that chieftain's clan, and, having been introduced in an off-hand way to several under chiefs who were hanging about, Lochiel gave some orders in Gaelic, and then left Scott, with an intimation that he hoped not to be long. In a few seconds an upturned barrel was spread with a meal

consisting of the remains of a haunch of
venison and a quaich of usquebaugh, a liquor
which, it may be mentioned, was even at that
date quite or almost entirely unknown in
many parts of the lowlands. Scott had certainly seen and tasted it before, but always
an adulterated drink, which passed current in
Edinburgh for the genuine Highland article.
When therefore, being very thirsty, he gulped
down a couple of mouthfuls of the liquid fire,
it was with a yell of savage fury that he
dashed the drinking vessel to the ground, and
swore in oaths, both loud and deep, that he would
be revenged for what he seemed to think an ill-
timed practical joke. The surrounding Highlanders at first could scarcely forbear a smile
at Scott's misfortune, but their innate sense of
politeness restrained them from laughing out-
right, a piece of bad manners which Scott,
who had consorted all his life with people
who boasted of their civilisation, seemed to
expect would follow as a matter of course.
There is no question, had laughter followed
Scott's misadventure, something else of a more
serious nature would have succeeded; but the
ex-smuggler's volley of curses died away,

apparently from very inanition or lack of appro-
priateness.

Cursing is a consuming fire which requires
fuel, and in this case even the dullest wit
could have recognised that his own greed had
been the cause of the *contretemps*. Besides
this, Scott felt that his method of expressing
his sentiments was not suited to the company, and
wisely commenced to try instead to suit himself
to his surroundings. The resolution was further
strengthened when one of his new companions
apologised to Scott in broken English for the
mishap.

"She pe vary sorry for ta whisky, she pe
so strong whateffer, she shall see if the shentle-
man's no can have ta claret drink."

To which our hero mumbled some sort of
an answer, and without further ado set to
with his case knife, and made a hearty breakfast off the venison. He had newly washed
this down with a copious draught of excellent
claret, when a courier appeared with a message for
Scott to accompany him back to the Prince's tent.

The audience that was granted was short,
but satisfactory. The Prince, who appeared
to be thoughtful, with an almost melancholy

expression of face, received his new recruit
with that dignity and courteousness of manner
for which he was famed, and by which he
gained no small share of popularity during
his brief career in this country. "I am pleased,"
his highness said, "to see that the Borders
are with us, and I trust many more will join
our army from that quarter: I thought," he
continued, "that Laidlay had been an older
man than yourself—perhaps there are two
of the same name?" This query at once
showed that Prince Charles was well acquainted
with particulars of the inhabitants of the
domains he claimed, and even knew to address
holders of land, not by their own names, but
that of their estates, as was the custom in
Scotland.

As a matter of fact, having this knowledge,
he was not at all satisfied in his own mind
that Scott was the man he represented himself
to be. The latter's reply, however, seemed
to satisfy him; he was Armstrong the younger;
a kindly inquiry for the elder of that name,
and a sly hint that a Border chieftain might
have been expected with a goodly following
at his heels, concluded the audience, after which

the newly made soldier had plenty of opportunity to iuspect the camp at his leisure. The
spot it occupied was close to the village of
Duddingston, and it was here, it may be
recollected, the Highlanders, after marching
through Edinburgh, rested until they were given
the word to march and engage the English
soldiers at Prestonpans.

Our hero was no soldier, but the disorder of
the camp and the pitiful state of the men, made
him stare in positive astonishment. The Highlanders were of low stature, dirty, and scared
looking, and although the officers were undeni-
ably gentlemen, their authority over the rank
and file seemed to be in a minus quantity during
the several days of weary waiting that followed.

When, however, the word of command went
forth to march to the field of battle, then all
became alacrity and cheerfulness. The Highlander loved that part of the programme, but, if
we except plunder, no other. The further he
left his native hills behind him, so did his
loyalty to his chief decrease, until, as every
school boy knows, the cause was lost, and the
hopes of the Stuarts dashed for ever, through
the greed, jealousy, and want of any approach

to discipline among these men, whose only objects in leaving their glens and hills were purely selfish, and did not include the slightest feeling of genuine loyalty towards the Prince.

The details of the battle of Prestonpans which took place are well known ; how, at the first rush of the Highlanders with their claymores, the infantry flung down its arms, mostly undischarged, and fled in confusion. Wild panic and dread possessed the red coats, and no persuasions or threats on the part of their officers—or a few of them it should be said, for many, including General Cope, were as frightened as the meanest private—could make them stand and face the enemy. The dragoons, under Colonels Whitney and Gardiner, attempted to charge, but wheeled immediately and rode off in the direction of Dolphingston. Colonel Gardiner endeavoured to rally his men, but to no purpose, only eleven following him back to the charge, in which he was cut down by a broadsword.

It was our friend's lot to march with the division of the army that was intended to turn the left flank of the enemy, but, having over-marched itself, it stumbled upon a few companies that were guarding the baggage in a small enclosure near Cockenzie, and speedily acquired both the companies and the baggage by right of conquest.

Scott had made **very** good friends with **two** or three of the Highland chieftains, and with them, **when the success all** along **the line of the** Prince's forces **was** ascertained, adjourned **to a** tavern that was not far distant.

Here **it** was deemed **both** necessary and expedient to bespeak an early and plentiful dinner, **and to** Scott, as knowing **best** the ways **of Lowland landladies, was** deputed **the** duty **of** ordering **the feast.** As the landlord had hidden himself on the **approach of the dreaded High-**landers, his goodwife, " Lucky Tamson," met the newly arrived guests at the threshold **and** showed them **to the best room.**

She **was a stout** buxom wife **of** thirty **or a** little **over, and in** attending upon her customers did not attempt to disguise her contempt and scorn for the faction which they represented. To Scott **her face was** quite familiar, but he did **not bestow many** thoughts upon that fact. He informed her that the party wished to partake of a substantial dinner, and until it was ready she had better bring in some of her best wine.

Upon receiving this order, instead of retiring, so as to get the repast ready, Lucky Thomson seated herself on a chair that was near the open door of the room, and taking up the lower edge of her apron, and running the seam through the fingers of one hand until she held it by the two bottom corners, she cast a scornful glance at her guests, and uttered in perfect unconcern the following query :—

"An' wha, may I speer, is tae pay me ma reck'nin'?"

The meaning of this was not caught by the Highlanders, but it was different with Scott, who, turning red with passion at the insult, as in his pride he considered it, he commanded her to obey his orders instantly, or it would be "worse for her!"

"Maybe it wull, an' maybe it wunna, ma man; but I'se no budge frae here till I ken where I'm tae get ma siller! Mind! I ken mair aboot ye than may be ye're thinkin' on."

One of the Highlanders, grasping her meaning, cried out in a shrill voice: "Fat is tat? does she no tak us to be shentlemens, effery one of us whateffer!" He had scarcely stopped speaking, when a hoarse whisper from some one outside the door, and out of sight, was heard:

" Tut, wumman! come awa', or we'll a' be killed! What does it maitter for the price of a denner?"

" G'wa oot o' sicht,"—an unnecessary piece of admonition; this from the landlady; " G'wa oot o' sicht if yer feared for thae Hieland traitors; but as sure as I'm Betsy Tamson, I'll no stir oot o' this till I ken I'm tae be paid;" to emphasise which ultimatum, she folded her bare arms upon her ample breasts in token of defiance.

By this time, however, one of the Highlanders had slipped from the room; and, after the sound of a slight scuffle in the passage, re-entered, dragging in the landlord, whose abject fear and trembling limbs were in the most powerful, as well as ludicrous, contrast to the deportment of his wife. " *Weak*" woman sat scornfully unconcerned, while " *strong* " man fell trembling on his knees, imploring the company not to visit his wife's sins on him.

" Dinna mind her, gentlemen! dinna mind her! I'll get ye yer dinners, het an' smokin'; she deserves to be punished, but dae it lichtly,

an' I'll dae onything ye like. And mind its no
ma daein she's that way !"

Several voices were now raised, and the party
speaking together at the other end of the room,
various plans of action were suggested.

It was quite plain, conquerors though they
were, their commands were unavailing. They
could have ransacked the house, and plundered
it to their hearts' content, but that was not what
they desired. Their souls thirsted and hungered
for a well-cooked and plentiful dinner, which,
however, Will. Scott loudly expostulated against
paying for, especially after the way they had
been defied.

The Highlanders, however, were unanimously
of opinion that they were bound in honour to
pay for what they got ; so one of them addressed
Lucky Thomson :

" Shentlemans will pay for ta dinner."

" Very weel, ma man ; when I see yer money
ye'll get yer dinner."

This led to a guinea being deposited in the
landlady's hand, who in a moment altered her
demeanour, without losing in any degree her
appearance of scornful regard.

Just as her husband was going to address the

party again, she caught him a cuff over the head, and ordered him to get out, a command he obeyed with alacrity, while the whole party were so much overcome with the absurdity of the situation, as to burst out into an unrestrained roar of laughter, which lasted until the arrival of Lucky Thomson with a supply of excellent claret.

The inn in which we are now supposed to be seated in company with Will. Scott and his newly made friends, was not by any means of the first class. This was shown by several customs, once universal, but fast disappearing in the better class of houses of public resort in 1745. Along with the claret one glass was set upon the table, which went round with the bottle, and was deemed an ample supply of crystal. In this case it had not had time to go round very often, when the door was opened, and there entered the landlady and her husband, ths latter of whom, as the result of a little domestic argument down stairs, appeared with his head bound round with a towel. Each carried a steaming dish. The one, a huge tureen, contained a savoury mixture of leeks, curley greens, parsnips, and a brace of fowls, all floating about in about a couple of gallons

of soup or kail, and the other a pair of sheep's
heads, plucks, and trotters, boiled with parsnips
and parsley, all piled up in a pewter platter
nearly three feet in diameter. Fingers in those
days were much in request, forks but little. In
fact, even so late as the date of this tale, people
who had acquired the habit of using such aids
to eating, seldom travelled without carrying
with them a fork, spoon, and knife in a shagreen
case; their chances of finding them in places
of public entertainment being but slender. Our
company, who by this time were all greedily
snuffing up the sweet savour of the viands
before them, were not so well equipped, but
each one carried his own knife, which, aided
by the ready response of the first finger and
thumb of the left hand, speedily transferred
large quantities of the delicacies from the dishes
into their various mouths. After the more solid
foods had been despatched in this way, an attack
was made on the broth, by means of thick horn
spoons, and then, satisfied and content, the bottle
was put under contribution.

During the progress of the feast, the landlady
was assisted in the waiting by her daughter, a
budding beauty of about sixteen, who dis-

played, despite a coarse and ill-fitting dress, a
figure of rare beauty. She had, in addition, fine
black eyes, raven hair, and, what made her
presence still more agreeable, a coy and attractive
manner. As the wine circulated, it became
evident that she had made an impression on
more than one of the manly hearts in the company, and her health was repeatedly pledged in
deep draughts of wine.

Presently two other Highland gentlemen
joined the gathering. Both were considerably
over sixty years of age, the one almost a
giant in height, with legs like whipping posts,
while the other was under medium height, but of
enormous bulk, his calves being more like
small barrels than anything else. Another
point of contrast between the two was, that,
while the former was perfectly sober, it could
easily be seen that he of the Falstaffian dimensions had been imbibing well if not wisely.
Both, however, were merry enough, and as a
piper had accompanied them, they insisted upon
having a dance. The roof of the room was not
much more than seven feet in height, so our
friend of the long proportions, in his jumps
during the reel, was frequently in danger of either

damaging it or his head. His shorter friend,
notwithstanding his unwieldy proportions, displayed much wildness in his movements, and
the whole scene became so irresistibly comic
that Kate, for such was the name of Lucky
Thomson's daughter, fell a-laughing, and not
being able to check herself, ran off. This
prevented her getting what was termed her
second course of kisses, although she had en-
dured the first—a loss which the two elderly
warriors aforementioned swore they could not
permit her to sustain, as they each would follow
her down stairs, and make it up to her. The
stout gentleman declared that his friend had
nothing to do with it, while the tall Highlandman contended that he alone would go in the
quest. Several other voices were raised, but
did not get much of a hearing. Swords were
drawn, and blood might have followed, had an
incident not occurred which effectually dispelled
all thoughts of jealousy about Kate. This
was nothing less than the giving way of the
supports of the floor, and the subsidence of
the entire party, amid dust and rubbish incon-
ceivable, into an apartment some ten feet
below !

The crazy joists of the floor had been no match for the dancing and stamping of the eight heavy men, who were now struggling and roaring to free themselves from the debris. Blinded as they were with the dust, and not knowing where the exit from their dungeon lay, their case was certainly far from pleasant. However, in due course the atmosphere cleared sufficiently for them to see the form of the landlady at the door of the room above, from which they had just descended in so unexpected a manner. She was gesticulating wildly and making no secret of the delight she felt at their discomfiture. She was too avaricious and cunning a woman not to see in their misfortune a chance of improving her good fortune, and let them very quickly know that, until she received a considerable sum of money to pay for the damage, she would ignore all appeals and entreaties for means whereby they might effect their escape.

CHAPTER IV.

THE writer does not wish to appear unkind in thought or deed, but it is necessary at this stage to leave our Border friend 'and his Highland acquaintances in the uncomfortable position that has just been described and to travel back, with double quick speed, across the Soutra Hill, and over the bonny Tweed as far as the Cleekim Inn ; for several important events had happened in that district since the evening that the beacon fires blazed forth their message of war to all the land.

Helen Kenway was a sensible business woman, who had had too large an experience of smugglers in general, and Will. Scott in particular, to be much put about at the abrupt departure of the lawless band on the evening that opened our tale. They might come back or they might not that would altogether

D

depend on circumstances. If they did come back, they would in all probability pay their reckoning; but, although, to a woman in her state of comparative poverty, the amount was considerable, it troubled her not very much. Helen possessed, blissfully unconscious although she was of the fact, the secret of never crying over spilt milk. What was done was done, and would not be mended by any lamentations or whines, however much the results of past foolishness and misfortunes might be lessened by resolute and firm reforms in the present and the future. This is philosophy, and although belonging to a school not over popular at the present day, is full of truth—for some philosophy is not only truthful but *true*. What really troubled Helen more than even her unpaid reckoning, was the indifferent and almost surly manner in which, during his recent as well as several former visits, Will. Scott had behaved towards her. Like the lady on Soutra Hill, she saw the change in his manner, but unlike the other she did not know or even imagine the cause. However, she busied herself day by day with her various duties, which were not onerous, and the few stray customers she entertained at her caravansary would have detected no change in her manner had they looked for it.

It was some four or five days after the departure of the smugglers already recorded that Helen Kenway beheld a mounted band of men coming from the south towards her house. Standing at her door, she was obliged to shade her eyes with her hand against the almost horizontal rays of the setting sun.

" Quick, quick," she cried, as turning into the house she busied herself putting things in their places, and making such preparations as landladies only know or understand. " Quick, quick, Marget, there's the awfae'st pack o' them comin' frae Lessuden I'se seen thae years ! "

The person addressed, a woman perhaps ten or fifteen years the other's senior, came hurriedly forth from an inner den or apartment, busily wiping her hands upon a coarse and exceedingly sombre-looking apron. Judging from the hue of the former, she did not seem to have been washing them, unless indeed, the latter had subsequently communicated to them something of its own peculiar shade; however, the action seemed rather to be resorted to from force of habit, and in common with a peculiar phrase of speech that she immediately gave vent to, was practised upon all and sundry occasions. "Gud a mercy! isn't this awfu'?" It was uttered most distinctly in a tone of a query, but that any reply was expected was not indicated by either look or action on her part.

Presently, however, Helen emerged from a trap-door communicating with the cellar, whither she had gone for a supply of liquor, and without pausing, began.

"Ay! there's abune twenty if there be ane, an' though they're no up tae the river yet, there's some o' them, I'm michty sure, I've seen no lang syne!"

"Gud a' mercy! isn't that awfu'?"

While a litany-like dialogue as above was going forward within the tavern, the cavalcade of horsemen which had given rise to it, slowly approached by the broad Roman road that led through Ancrum forest from the north. The horsemen had crossed the Teviot which, at that particular spot, glides smoothly and peacefully between its grassy banks. The scene is one eminently calculated to suggest and stimulate thoughts of a gentle and soothing nature, especially as witnessed on such an evening, for, in addition to the pastoral beauty of the river, with its undulating reaches and sloping banks of verdure, the rays of the sun, that had half-blinded Helen Kenway as she gazed northward, were coming slightly from the rear of the riders, and were shining in all their glory upon the white front of the inn and dark setting of the pine trees behind. The red trunks and branches of the trees blazed out like initial letters among the more sombre text in an illuminated missal, deep red on a dark ground.

"This is the inn, sir," said one of the men, addressing a tall rider, who appeared, by his dress and bearing, to be of higher rank than the rest.

"So I supposed," replied he addressed; "but it is not here, but in Jedburgh, we will catch the murderer."

"'Deed, sir," observed the other, " ye're a clever man, an' it wasna' mony that could hae planned yon trap we laid at Soutra; ye'll excuse me for sayin' sae, but ye'll be a cleverer man still if ye trap Wull Scott ance he's safe in Jeddart; but we'll see, we'll see!"

By this time the door of the inn was reached, and the leader called out, "If any of you wish refreshment it will be brought out, we have little time to spare." Saying which he himself dismounted, and calling on the man with whom we have just made some acquaintance, by the name of Montgomery, to follow him, he · entered and asked Helen Kenway, who met him at the door, if she were the landlady.

"That I am, sir, and richt welcome ye are; this way, sir." So saying, she led him to the "best" room.

"Will you please," he said, "let my men be served; Montgomery, who has dismounted, will carry the liquor to them, and bring me yourself a pint of claret; we are in somewhat of a hurry, and I wish to have a few minutes' conversation with you if you will afford it."

There was a certain air of superiority in this man's manner that at once demanded respect, and Helen, somewhat puzzled at the whole affair, curtseyed and left the room. She hurriedly instructed Marget to serve Montgomery, and contrived, while she procured the wine for the "captain," as she termed him, to convey to her subordinate an elaborate and somewhat expanded account of what that individual had said to her, eliciting in reply the familiar "Gud a' mercy, that's awfu'."

"Will you be seated for a minute," queried the "captain," as Helen re-entered the room with his wine. "I wish to inform you in the first place that I am a Custom House officer, and have arrested a gang of smugglers, whom I am conveying to Jedburgh." He paused for a moment and Helen most ingeniously raised her two hands as if in astonishment, and exclaimed, "That's maist awfu'!"

"Now," he continued, "I've no doubt you know these men." "Me," cried Helen, apparently lost in astonishment. "Yes; but of course I don't suppose for a moment you knew them to be smugglers." He said this with a kindly smile that at once won a path into the heart of the landlady, and he continued: "Now, the fact of the matter is, one of them has escaped, and he, above all others, I wanted to secure."

"No Wull Scott, was it?"

The captain did not let it be seen that he noticed her betrayal of knowledge of the members of the gang, but went on: "Yes, Scott is the man, and I am most anxious to secure him."

"'Deed, then, captain, I'm thinking ye'll be a clever man if ye catch Wull Scott; but what dae ye want wi' me, may I ask? I've naething tae dae wi' him."

"You shall hear; regarding this Scott, I may or I may not catch him; I shall do my best, you may be sure; but I must say I am surprised to hear that you think such a great deal of him."

This was cunningly put, in order to find out if she had any interest in or affection for the man, for on the chance of this all the officer's hopes of getting information from her rested.

"'Deed, and if that's a' ye have got tae say tae me, I micht as weel be attending tae ma business."

"Not so fast, my good lady, not so fast; what I said was little more than a jest; I know very well that a woman of your sense would have little reason to think anything of a mere smuggler, especially when you have charms, excuse me for saying so, which would give you a choice of better men; why"—the flattery was working—"why, a lady of your attractions would never bother her head about a man who is as free of his attentions as any common sailor, who, they say, has a wife in every port."

"It's no true," screamed out Helen Kenway,

and disagreeably awakened from the sweet sense of being flattered by a particularly good-looking man; " It's no true ; I'll no believe it."

" Alas ! but I can prove it, prove that he is unworthy your regard; listen." Then he of the dark red hair and black eyes recounted to Helen Kenway all, and a little more, than he knew about Scott's appointment with the mistress of Carfrae Mill Inn, of his affection for her of Soutra Hill, and sundry other particulars, all mixed with sly flattery, the result being that Helen, mentally comparing these statements with things she had herself recently observed in Scott's behaviour, jumped to the conclusion that the stranger's story was true, and had it been possible for her to betray his whereabouts to the "captain," she would have done so with a feeling of malicious glee.

He, for his part, could easily see that Helen was telling him the truth, when she declared she had not set eyes on the man he wanted since he had deserted the gang. Satisfied that he would not get further information, he paid her for her liquor, and mounting his horse rode on in front of his men up the steep road to the south.

Helen naturally had much afterwards to tell Marget, who, at proper intervals, interjected her favourite exclamation, and when she got an opportunity, informed Helen she had heard much discontent expressed by the Custom House officers, whose chief had dismounted for his refreshment, while they had been obliged to partake of theirs on horseback, a thing they had never done before, especially at the Cleekim Inn; but the "captain" was a new officer, who would no doubt learn his duty in time. The ordinary run of Custom officers met their foes on an equal understanding in at least one thing, namely, that no opportunity for a comfortable halt should be lost, even when something more important was in progress. The night was getting late, and as Marget let the massive oaken bar into its standirons, she might have been heard to remark, "Gud a' mercy, it's maist awfu'!"

CHAPTER V.

To the throats of the sturdy Highlandmen who were imprisoned in the lower flat of Lucky Thomson's inn, the dust was not at all pleasant; accustomed to the pure and bracing air of the mountains, the scent of the heather and the countless flowering plants that grew wild in their native land, stale mortar, dust, and the smell of dry rot, all of them in profusion, were not congenial.

Great, therefore, was their wrath, and loud their language, at what appeared to them to be unnecessary delay on the part of the landlady to release them.

It was while the flow of Gaelic conversation was at its height that Will. Scott, quietly sitting on a broken beam, bethought him that some of the contents of the apartment in which he had so suddenly discovered himself imprisoned, were not altogether unfamiliar. Not that there was much

light to notice anything by; but at his feet there
stood a keg, and upon it a mark he knew as well
as Jedburgh Cross. It was a keg of smuggled
brandy. Without a moment's reflection he approached as near under where Lucky Thomson
stood as circumstances would permit, and speaking rapidly, and in a tone calculated to reach her
ear, but not those around him, he said, " Gie me
a rope and let me up; if ye dinna, I'll let the
Excise ken this place is fu' o' smuggled gear."
At first the amazon above pretended to disregard his remarks, but a quiet warning that he
would proceed to smash up the casks that were,
as yet, mostly covered with rubbish, and so
waste their contents, brought her to her senses,
and she at once proceeded to lower a rope into
the hands of the ex-smuggler. No sooner had
this been done than the Highlanders, with one
common impulse, made a rush for the means of
escape, but Scott, fruitful as ever of resource,
said, " Gentlemen, gie me leave first to gang up;
I hae contrived tae humbug the wife, and she'll
let me ascend. She says if the rest try she'll
lowse the rope! "

The logic of necessity is generally convincing,
and so our Highland friends quietly stood by

and beheld their brother in arms, but stranger in blood, ascend the rope and stand safely on *terra firma* above. They very naturally expected that "Laidlay," as they called him, would set about securing their escape as his first duty; but in this they were mistaken.

It may have been gathered from an expression of Lucky Thomson's, recorded some pages back, that she had an acquaintance with Scott's identity. This was the case; but although she had about the most sufficient reason a woman can have for remembering a man, it had been so long since she had last seen him, some seventeen years, and the curious circumstances under which she now met him, that she had not absolutely made up her mind on the point until he betrayed himself by showing his acquaintance with the private marks used by smugglers. These were only known to that fraternity and the Excise officers.

She knew Scott to be none of the latter, and once she had settled he was one of the other class, she had no difficulty in fixing his identity.

"So they ca' ye Laidlay, ma fine cock o' the walk; and ye're galavanting as a Hielander, and a gentleman forsooth; guidness, but ye've got a maist uncommon neck, and nae mistake. Dinna try ony o' yer pranks on wi' me; I mind ye fine, an' I'll gie ye a bit o' ma mind, Wull Scott, afore ye gang."

"For guidness sake, wumman, dinna speak sae loud."

"Oh! ye're feared yer freends 'll hear; is that it, ma bonny man? an' supposin' I just tell them wha ye are th' noo, ye wudna like that, I'm thinkin.'"

"If ye dare, ye bitch, I'll strangle ye."

"Will ye, though? I'm thinkin' ye'll dae less. Come ben here, I've something tae say tae ye." Saying which, she retired with Scott into a small apartment, and closed and locked the door.

Lucky Thomson was, as we have seen, a woman of no ordinary capacity. In addition to the business of a country inn, she carried on an extensive smuggling trade, and hitherto had been able to completely defy all the efforts of the authorities to find her out. Her house was perfectly well known to be a storehouse for immense quantities of contraband goods, but though it had been watched for weeks, and even months together, never a clue had been got as to how the business was carried on. The officers had made sudden and unexpected descents upon the premises, only to find the ordinary routine of her business being carried on quietly and steadily.

On one occasion they discovered the landlord and a well known smuggler drinking together, in evident great friendship. There was nothing incriminating in the circumstance, however, and so the officers joined them with the hope that the weak-kneed host would perhaps divulge some secret while in his cups. In this they were disappointed, as they had been in all their other schemes to make a seizure.

Lucky Thomson was a sister of Helen Kenway, and had met Scott many years before on the banks of the Teviot. In fact, there had not been wanting sundry love passages in their acquaintance at that time, carried on by him with reckless indifference to anybody's feelings or interests except his own, and with results which will prove of the deepest importance to some of the characters introduced into this tale. Whatever her thoughts had then been towards him, it was business, not love, that occupied her mind as she stood facing Scott in the little parlour.

She had a proposition to make to him, and without any hesitation she proceeded.

"Wull Scott, ye see there are fifty packages doun yonder. The deil tak' thae Hieland beasts that cam jumpin' on ma floor tea break it in! Noo they maun a' be lifted, an' at ance. They murderin' thieves 'll be awa' in twa three days, an' then the gaugers 'll be doun on me."

"What dae ye want me tae dae?"

"Yon cellar has twa doors: yin intae here," and she pointed to a corner of the room where an old broken spinet stood; "and anither through a lang passage tae a house awa' doun the brae. I'll let thae deevils oot, an' when ye hear them gang, you gae intae the cellar. I'll show ye the door, an' awa alang tae Biddy Ferguson, wha keeps the house at the ither end. Tell her it's a' richt till Monday; and then she'll tell ye whaur tae gang an' what tae dae. Thae barrels maun be removed at ance."

"An' suppose I refaise?"

"Then I'll gang an' tell yer freends wha ye are, an' that ye wanted me tae let ye steal their horses an' mak' off; an' I'm thinkin' ye'll no like that, ma cock o' Jeddart!"

The gentleman so addressed did not feel tempted by the alternative; for a moment he contemplated putting a pistol bullet through the woman's head, but it was only for a moment. There is a peculiar something about some people, that seems to raise them above the slightest chance of danger. The bravest, as well as the craftiest, quail before their glance, and the boldest schemes that can be devised become instantly blunted and useless.

So Scott found it as he met the gaze from the eyes confronting him, and he submissively acquiesced in her proposal. Accordingly he was shown through a small door, cunningly contrived in the wall of the room in which the above dialogue had taken place.

Left in a dark passage for some time, his feelings were not, by any means, so elated as they had been during the earlier portion of the day. He had been trapped as completely by this woman, as if he had been a green youth; not only had he lost for ever any chance of promotion in the Prince's army, but, worse by far, he had drifted back into his old course of life, without having been able to do anything to prevent it. There could be no mistaking

E

Lucky Thomson's meaning. She held a power over him in knowing who and what he was. There was another hold she had upon him, and that of the most important nature; but, in the mean time, she did not bring it to the surface. For the present she was using her advantage over Scott to enable her successfully to get her stock of contraband goods safely conveyed from her house, before it was possible she should receive a visit from the Custom House officers. He was to be her instrument in this matter, and he knew he dare not dream of thwarting her, or else worse might follow.

"Bah!" at last he exclaimed, "what for did I no put a bullet through her heid? It's ower late noo though—for there's nae sayin' what she's been tellin' thae Hielanders, an' they're no sae easy argued wi'; for they're a' gentlemen, an' think a michty lot o' honour. They wudna be pleased either that I hae been passin' mysel' off as yin o' themsel's; an' besides, they'll think I hae played them the traitor, in no helpin tae get them oot o' yon hole."

As for Lucky Thomson, on leaving the prisoner in the secret passage, she hastened to those in the cellar, and was by no means pleas-

antly impressed with the nature of the salutation she got. It took the form of a couple of
pistol balls, which whistled past her ear, and
went "pug" into the wood-work in the passage.

"Hech! sirs, but that's ill requital for me as
is gettin' ye a ledder tae get oot wi';" and without further parley, she produced and lowered a
short ladder into the cellar, up which it did not
take many seconds for the imprisoned Highlanders to mount. To a woman possessed of
less resource and daring than the mistress of the
inn, the scene that followed would have been
full of danger. Highland blood runs quickly,
and Highland breasts can ill brook the thought
of being taken advantage of. However, Lucky
Thomson very easily turned their wrath from
herself to her luckless captive Scott, whom she
accused of being a spy. She said he had
endeavoured to bribe her to leave his former
companions where they were locked up, either
to starve, or else await the departure of the
Prince's troops, and then have them given up
as prisoners to the Royalists.

In time they not only believed her, but paid her
handsomely with some of the gold they had stolen
that morning. After a drink of wine to wash down

the dust, they mounted their horses and rode off
at double quick speed in pursuit of the supposed
spy, whom Lucky Thomson had indicated as
having gone in a direction quite different from
what she knew he would take. But one of their
number remained behind. It was the gentleman
of the fat legs, who declared he was "too much
hurt whateffer" to travel. His wounds seemed
to be internal and in the neighbourhood of the
heart, for, as he sat in the kitchen, his eyes
never ceased following the movements of Kate
as she busied herself with the household duties.
When the mother was present, the cunning old
Highlander was careful to address his remarks
entirely to her, although it was quite evident,
from a variety of nods and winks, that Kate and
he had been holding converse when left alone,
and that their discourse had led to some mutual
understanding, which might have been guessed
at by any one who had taken the trouble to
observe their actions.

Meantime Scott had been shown by his captor
to the entrance of the subterranean passage, and
duly instructed by his taskmistress in his duties.
The first of these was to find his way to the
other end, and await the advent of nightfall in

the cottage of Biddy Ferguson, who of course
was the landlady's agent in the contraband
business, and by whose aid the latter had been
enabled to carry on her trade, even while the
Custom House officers were actually staying in
the inn! When it was quite dark, and the
coast clear, Scott was to make his way to Leith,
and there deliver a brief message to a certain
merchant. The reasons Lucky Thomson had
been anxious to select Scott for her messenger
were twofold. Firstly, he was a smuggler, and
so might be relied upon on the principle of
" Honour among thieves;" and, secondly, being
acquainted with the whereabouts of the Highlanders, and knowing their pass-words, would be
able to reach his destination where another
would probably have failed.

Now it so happened that, upon the evening of
that eventful day, as Lucky Thomson was busy-
ing herself within doors, and congratulating herself upon the success of her plan, she became
suddenly aware of the absence of her daughter
Kate, whom she could not find anywhere.
For a young girl to be amissing at such a
time, when an army of Highland savages was
within the distance of a mile or two, was,

to say the least of it, alarming, and the mother knowing the girl's somewhat flighty nature, as well as the unprincipled nature of the men by whom she would likely be taken, fairly lost all control of herself in her mad grief and rage. That she believed within her own mind that Kate had not left the house unwillingly, was evident from the nature of the expletives that encumbered her soliloquies. The consternation that followed the discovery of Kate's absence seemed, on the other hand, to prove beneficial to the condition of the gentleman with the fat legs, for he got up and volunteered his aid to find her. Accordingly he sallied forth into the darkness, and in not more than a quarter of an hour returned out of breath, and in evident excitement.

His tale was brief. He had seen Scott, or Laidlay as he called him, riding away, with the girl holding on behind. He had been unable to stop the runaways, as he himself was unmounted, but he would mount his own horse now, and he would find the young lady, "whateffer." And find her he undoubtedly did, waiting patiently but nervously for him within a short distance from her mother's inn. It was perfectly true that he had seen Scott riding away, and much astonished, if not alarmed, he was at the sight; but Kate was not with the ex-smuggler. Her present waiting-place had been carefully planned during the intervals of the day, when her mother had been busy with Scott about her smuggling affairs. The Highlandman's tongue had lured this silly young bird from the nest, chiefly by promising to let her see all the glories of the Prince's camp, and the gaieties of Edinburgh. And, so as to make his retreat both more secure and his route less suspected, the crafty old monster had put the blame on Scott, while the landlady, knowing that gentleman of old, readily believed the worst of him. Poor woman, like so many more of her sex, she trusted for redress to the very man who was injuring her.

As for Kate—well, she was intoxicated with the idea of seeing so many brave sights on the morrow. That is what Master Fox talked to her about, and so made her forget the roost she had left to go along with him. Is it worth while inquiring whether he kept his word? Events will show.

CHAPTER VI.

In order to elude any possible vigilance on the part of the Prince's sentries, Will. Scott made a wide detour to the south, and passing the west side of the hill that lies directly to the north of Corstorphine, entered, as the sun rose the following morning, a little house of entertainment that stood upon the thickly wooded banks of the river Almond, just where it is spanned by the bridge of historic as well as romantic memory.

He had quite made up his mind not to take the message that had been entrusted to him, and at the same time he meant, now that his further connection with the army was impossible, to endeavour, by altering his appearance as much as possible, and making himself out to be a gentleman, to escape detection, and still enjoy all the pleasures of life in the capital. The gold that had so

luckily come into his possession was still safe, and carefully hidden on his person. If nothing else should turn up in the course of a month or two, he would embark in some vessel at Leith, and, as to destination, that mattered little to him. The world was his oyster, to open with either his sword or any other instrument that might lie nearest his hand. Before entering Edinburgh, however, he thought it would be well for him to lie quiet until the Highlanders marched south, and his intention now was to remain in the inn at which he had arrived. Finding, however, its proximity to the main road not at all to his liking, he removed to the small fishing village of Cramond, at the mouth of the river, where, for the matter of a few weeks, let us leave him to the contemplation of the ebbing and flowing tide upon that immense stretch of sand that joins Cramond Island to the mainland at one state of the water, and removes it over a mile from the shore at the other.

The capture that Thomas Mason, for such was the name of the red-headed and black-eyed Custom House officer, had made was distinctly important. How much so he himself did not

know until his arrival in Jedburgh. It led to
the seizure of a large quantity of contraband
goods, and supplied clues to various ramifications
of the trade, that promised Mason work for
months to come. As already mentioned, Jedburgh at this time, and for many years afterwards, was the centre of a most extensive and
profitable smuggling trade, which had grown to
such proportions that the authorities at Edinburgh and Berwick had determined upon using
the most stringent measures for its repression.
For this purpose they had appointed Mason to
take command of the whole district, and spare
neither expense nor trouble in bringing the
offenders to justice. He entered upon his new
duties with an enthusiasm and determination
that fairly astonished the rank and file of his
subordinates from Leith to Berwick. The habits
of these men, as already hinted at, had been
of a nature scarcely calculated to strike
terror into the hearts of the lawbreakers, and
it was even suspected that cases of mutual understanding between the officers and the smugglers
were not unfrequent. A quiet hint not to be in
a certain district on such and such a day, and
a substantial present accompanying it, had more

than likely been given on more occasions than one, but over and above this, the government force was most inefficient, and its lack of discipline ill fitted it to cope with the fearless bands of smugglers with which it had to deal. Prompt action, and absolute devotion to duty, were the qualities that the new captain brought to bear upon the solution of the difficulty; with the immediate result that he was hated by his subordinates, and feared by his enemies.

In a short time, however, the former respected and reverenced him as an able and successful leader, the Soutra Hill exploit having something to do with the change of opinion. At the time, it was regarded as unprecedented for successful daring; only one man, perhaps, thought otherwise, and that was Mason himself, who looked upon the capture of Scott as of more importance than that of a hundred others of less prominence in the business.

Naturally, therefore, when he had arrived at Jedburgh, and done everything necessary for the moment, he turned his thoughts again towards Scott: following up every clue he could find that seemed likely to lead him to his intended captive.

That he was not in Jedburgh, was soon
evident. As to his presence in Edinburgh,
Mason was not at all certain, although information which he received from time to time seemed
to forbid any idea of it. Where therefore was
he to turn? The idea of the Prince's army
had occurred to him, but it did not seem a
likely refuge for a smuggler—nor would it have
been for an ordinary type of his class perhaps,
but Scott was an exceptional man, a fact not
yet fully known to Mason.

While he was chafing thus in uncertainty
as to how to act, some information was intercepted
by his men which compelled him to make a
sudden departure from Jedburgh, and hasten
towards an inn in Haddingtonshire, which he
had good reason to hope he would find filled
with a large quantity of contraband goods.
The hope of a great seizure is always dear
to the mind of an Excise officer, and so for the
moment Mason forgot his anxiety about the
whereabouts of Scott, and hastened his preparations. These did not take long, and, accompanied by half a dozen men, he was soon on
the road. He crested the hill that overlooked
the Cleekim Inn, and the sight of it recalled to

his mind the cause of his first visit there, and
without any definite object in view he ordered a
halt in front of its door.

"Richt prood am I tae see ye, Captain,"
exclaimed Helen Kenway; "an' what can I be
daein' for ye this day?"

"A drink for my men, mistress, and a word
with you." Saying which he entered the inn,
and in a few moments had heard from its
mistress the news that Scott had joined the
Prince's army, and had been last seen in the
tavern kept by her sister, Lucky Thomson, at
Tranent.

This information caused Mason to open his
eyes a good deal further than was their normal
condition, as he said, "Your sister, you say, has
an inn at Tranent. I intend to travel in that
direction, so I shall call; maybe I shall hear
something of this man; at any rate, I can take
her your compliments." Saying which he bade
her adieu, mounted his horse, and commanded
his followers to follow at their best speed.

Mason's thoughts were busy as he rode along.
This man Scott, whom it was his great endeavour
to secure, seemed to be of a different stamp to the
ordinary smuggler; or had he merely been driven to

join the rebels for fear of the consequences of his rash act at Soutra Hill? Then, this sister of the mistress of Cleekim. It was her house that he had discovered to be the head-quarters of a notorious gang that practised on the east coast. Evidently Scott had to do with that too, or else why his presence there? And then, Helen Kenway, was she engaged in the same trade in a wholesale way, or was her commerce with contraband goods limited to an occasional keg of brandy and the sheltering of smugglers who paid for her hospitality? However, he would find out, he doubted not, and that as soon as he had arrived at his destination; so putting spurs to his horse he galloped along in a manner that did not at all please his less enthusiastic followers.

When, on the following day, he neared the house of Lucky Thomson, Mason deployed his men so that at a given signal they would surround the house; no more mistakes of letting any one escape by back doors; and then he had time to speculate on the chances of capturing Scott along with the rest of the contraband goods he believed lay there concealed. The mistress of the inn had received no warning of his approach, Mason's movements were too quick for that, and her consternation when she found every door guarded and her house full of gaugers was complete. Had it not been for the mishap of the floor, the occurrence would not have put her much about. Her house had been descended upon before, and as already said, she had carried on her trade even under the very noses of the officers. Now she knew the full extent of her danger, but for all that she did not lose her self-possession or presence of mind for a moment.

"Weel, ma bonny men," was her salutation as they entered; "maybe ye'll be gude eneuch to say what's yer wull; I'm thinkin' ye're no sae weel mainnered as the Hielanders that were here sin syne."

Mason here came forward, and telling his men not to disperse, requested a word with her in private. "'Deed I'll gie ye nae words in private; if ye want ony liquor, Lucky Tamson's is coonted as gude as ye'll get atween this and the Mercat Cross o' Edinburgh."

"Mistress Thomson, we are here in the king's name, and so, as you disregard civility, I order you to do as I bid."

"Maybe, ma braw man, ye'll just tell me which king ye refer tae, for we've had twa kinds here lately, and by ma fegs the Hieland ane is the maist ceevil, and pays best."

This was a bold speech, but Lucky Thomson was a desperate woman, and recked little what she said so she could save her contraband goods; but her assurance availed her nothing with Mason. The tone of his commands demanded obedience, and in another minute the mistress of the inn was standing, sorely against her will, indignant and full of wrath, confronting him in the small chamber containing the spinet and the secret door.

"Now, my good woman," commenced the officer, in a perfectly good-natured and friendly voice, "I can quite understand that you do not care about giving this man up to me, nevertheless it has got to be done, and the sooner the better."

Interrupting him, she exclaimed in surprise, "Whae dae ye mean?" He proceeded quietly: "I am surprised, I must say, to find a woman of your good sense risking so much for the sake of a man who, after all, is quite unworthy of you or any decent woman; but remember, you are harbouring a traitor as well as a smuggler and a murderer as well, so I advise you as a friend to let me have him and we shall depart, and no more shall be said about it.   I will give you my word."

During this speech rage and resentment had given placé in the matron's bosom for genuine blank astonishment.   Her ideas were lost in bewilderment, and the power of speech seemed to have left her lips.

After waiting a few moments Mason continued, " You know, of course, of whom I speak, Will. Scott, the smuggler."   The scales fell from her eyes, and with a burst of passion she almost screamed in her rage.   " Wull Scott, the fause, dirty thief !   Me harbour Wull Scott, the mean, rascally scum !   Ye accuse me o' harbourin' siccan a man !   G'wa and find him as fast as ye like. I daur say ye're nae better than him yersel, and ken fine whaur he's bidin'.   G'wa and bring me back ma dochter that he stole frae me !"   And so she raved for a good while, during which it became Mason's turn to be astonished.   He had firmly made up his mind that Scott was hiding there; anyway he risked the larger cast first, knowing how important it was to secure the man before the goods, and had hoped to gain his end by means of his tongue, a more useful and certain weapon, he had always found, than pistols

F

and swords. Now he saw his mistake. Clearly
Scott was not here, and this woman was apparently the last person in the world to harbour him if
he were! He waited patiently until her rage was
spent, politely apologised for having believed her
capable of sheltering such a notorious villain,
and then drew from her a long recital of the
events that followed the battle. In recounting
these she was careful, of course, to omit all mention of the floor falling in, and the fact of her
taking Scott into her confidence, and pressing
him into her service. She merely gave an ex-
aggerated account of the performances of the
Highlanders, and of Scott secretly decamping
with her daughter. "Then you have no clue,"
queried Mason, "as to their whereabouts now?"
But the question was unguardedly put. She
was quick-witted enough to see the advantage
of the possession, or even the supposed possession of knowledge, and in case of difficulties
preferred to keep her own counsel.

"An' may be, sir," she replied, "ye'll just tell
me what way ye speir?"

"Why; because he is a smuggler, a traitor
and a murderer. I told you so before."

"That's a' vera fine, but it's naething tae me.

Ye had a richt, I suppose, tae frichten everybody oot o' their seeven senses comin' here and demanding this and that, but I'm no compelled tae tell ye my thochts or what I ken, or what I dinna ken."

"But I have the power to arrest you for having harboured several of the rebels upon your own confession."

"Ay," she quickly rejoined, "an' ye had better arrest the hale o' Tranent, an' the Pans, no tae mention Musselburgh, and Edinburgh, for I'm thinkin' they are as muckle tae blame."

Mason could not very well get over this logic; and, for a moment, was puzzled what to say in reply, when she recommenced :—

"Noo, if that's a' ye hae tae say, ye had better gang the gate ye cam', an' leave dacent bodies tae get on wi' their wark."

His reply to this at once dispelled the hope she had been encouraging in her own mind, that Scott had been the sole object of his quest; for he quietly informed her the nature of his other duty. Then it was she cursed Scott to herself more deeply than before; for she blamed him as the indirect cause of the Highlanders invading her premises, and the subsequent accident to the floor, but for which she would have felt as secure as if there hadn't been a gill of "free" brandy in her house. And then, he had not only stolen her daughter, but had failed to deliver her message to the agent at Leith; had he done so, she might, by that time, have been safe. However, to surrender was not a part of her creed; so she merely replied to Mason's charge :

"There's plenty o' ye here, ye had better satisfy yersels; for I've nae doot ye're sae accustomed tae leein' yersels, that ye expec' every ither body tae dae the same!"

"*Now*," thought Mason, shall I strike a bargain, and let her off on condition she tells me where to find Scott? Yes, he resolved, I shall; but he reckoned without his hostess, who refused all conditions, and indignantly bade him go and search for himself. She was wise enough to see that she had still two chances left—the chance of him not discovering anything, and, secondly, her supposed knowledge of the whereabouts of Will. Scott.

Reluctantly, Mason ordered his men to search the house, which they did with right good will and very soon came to the door, now locked and nailed up, of the room that had been the scene of the recent accident.

" What's in here ? "

" Naething gude that I ken o'," replied Lucky Thomson, " it was nailit up years syne ; as there was gey queer things seen gaun' aboot at nichts, 'specially aboot the gloamin' time, just as it micht be the noo."

This statement checked in an instant a couple of officers who were on the point of smashing in the panels, but Mason was not to be so easily taken in, and seizing an axe, and calling on his men to support him, he wielded it with such a purpose that in less than a minute the fastening gave way, and with a crash and a shout he, it, and two of his men, all disappeared into the unknown depths beyond. It may well be supposed that the half hour that followed the sudden disappearance of Mason and the two men was one of great commotion in the inn. It will be remembered that the door which Mason had forced open was the one that admitted to what had been the best room of the house ; and that the floor having fallen in, as already described, the

Custom House officers fell headlong a depth of about ten feet. Mason being nearest the door fell first, the other two landed on top of him, and so considerably aggravated the disastrous result of his fall. When, finally, he was hauled out along with the other two, it was found that one leg and one arm were broken, and he had received in addition a severe scalp wound. He was accordingly carried up to bed. The other two men were little hurt, and they and their companions elected to remain on the premises until such time as they could receive instructions from Mason.

In the mean time, a surgeon had been got who made all right with their leader, enjoining that he should be kept perfectly quiet for the present.

This was an order the subordinates were not likely to disobey, as they found themselves comfortably ensconced, with nothing to do save "eat, drink, and be merry," never giving a thought to the reservation that "to-morrow we die."

In their minds, this act of Mason's did not add to any feelings of admiration they had previously felt for their chief. To be daring was one thing, but to tempt Providence with thrusting oneself into haunted rooms was another; and wild horses would not have drawn any one of them to inspect the unknown abyss that had caused the mishap.

Lucky Thomson was careful to encourage this superstition, and at the same time to have the doorway boarded up. On the principle that small things often gladden the heart when great sorrows oppress the mind, she was far from displeased that the band remained as guests in her house, when it became known to her that they were both prepared and willing to pay for what they received, and their demands, in the shape of liquid refreshments, were pretty considerable.

For nearly ten days after his accident Mason lay in a state of high fever, and unable to give the slightest attention to his work; but when he once began to mend his recovery was both rapid and complete, and in less than three weeks' time he was again going about, and anxious to be off and away so as to make up for lost time.

During his convalescence he had used every endeavour to make friends with the hostess of the inn, in the hope that he would obtain from her some information about Scott; but she, very wisely, maintained a discreet silence.

During the time of Mason's illness she had ample time to remove from her cellar all proof of her connection with the smuggling trade.

So, at last, with three weeks lost, and without even having made a seizure, Mason had to take his leave, a sadder but by no means a wiser man. He turned his horses' heads towards Edinburgh, where, in addition to getting through an accumulation of routine work, he never lost sight of his purpose to capture Will. Scott, if indeed that slippery individual was really in Edinburgh—a fact he was beginning to doubt, when an accident brought him face to face with the very man; but in such a manner that the encounter served no purpose.

> " Show his eyes, and grieve his heart,
> Come like shadows to depart."

CHAPTER VII.

WE shall now return to Will. Scott, who, having waited several weeks at Cramond with great discontent, at length judged it safe to re-enter the capital, which he found in a state of tranquility and order that he little expected would be the case, after it having been so recently occupied by a hostile army. The bulk of the inhabitants seemed to look upon the late incursion with perfect indifference. The merchants and workmen went about their daily occupations just as if nothing had happened, and although men were cautious in not expressing their opinions too freely, any one could see that the feeling of contempt with which they regarded this vast Jacobite expedition was supreme.

At " Fortune's Tavern," at which Scott chose to put up, our hero met with a gentleman who had travelled much, and who, unlike the natives, was very free of his opinion. " Why," said this worthy, "supposing they did reach London—which I may tell you they never will—well, what would happen? why, they would be lost. Lost, I tell you, sir. These savages would be rendered speechless with astonishment at what they saw, and in a few days it would be hard to find a single one of them."

"But," interjected Scott, when he was caught up by his friend, without allowing him to say another word. "Exactly. 'But' is the word. You were going to say what would their leaders be doing? Well, my friend, they would be left high and dry—their troops gone off to enjoy the various vices of the town, and with not a single man in sympathy with them. No, no! depend upon it, the people of England, as a body, do not like fighting and throat-cutting. It does not pay. They prefer making money. If you had seen these Highlanders you would have known I was right."

This latter remark was made without any change of voice, but an observant onlooker might have detected the stranger dart a searching look at Scott as he uttered the words, which almost resolved itself into a suspicion of a smile as the latter unguardedly said: "Oh! but I hae seen them, and I quite agree wi' ye."

"I didn't know," the stranger quietly re-marked, and immediately changed the subject.

Scott was not wanting in cunning, but his native abilities were not sufficient to carry him successfully through a career of deception. In the first place, he had never learned the golden rule of silence. Those who have important secrets to keep constantly make the mistake of volunteering information and, by forgetting what they have said, contradict themselves, with the result that they are suspected. Your old hand knows better, hearing everything and saying nothing—or at least confining his conversation exclusively to purely non-personal matters. Now Scott, upon his very first acquaintance, made over a friendly bottle with the stranger, had volunteered a long statement that he was the son of a small laird up Dumfries way, and that he had come to Edinburgh purely for pleasure. This was the worst policy, for it at once sug-gested to the other that not only was it not true, but that in making it Scott had something to conceal. Unfortunately for our hero, it was this gentleman's habit to suspect everybody. It was his business so to do, and through having an open, engaging manner, full of information and anecdote, being, in short, excellent company, he seldom had any difficulty in making crowds of acquaintances wherever he went, and many were the secrets and conspiracies that he got to the bottom of without ever showing his hand. He belonged to the secret police, and it was his duty to find out clues for others to work up and pounce upon the offenders when necessary. This was likely to be a busy season with him, for the Government was anxious to find out who among the apparently quiet and loyal portion of the population were mixed up in the rising. Those who had taken the field they knew how to deal with in good time; their hour would come; but, in the mean while, it was well to know more of the whereabouts and doings of the secret agents of the party. It was on this account that the stranger, whose name was Conway, determined to cultivate Scott's acquaintance, leading up gradually to the subject of the rebellion, and then, as we have seen, very easily getting a clue to that worthy's past.

As for our hero, blissfully unconscious that he had made any mistake, and being anxious above all things to enjoy to the full the pleasures of the town, he determined to lose no time in

altering his personal appearance as much as
possible. Having money in his pocket, this
was not difficult to do; and that the result
was entirely satisfactory, he was quite assured
after he had called and not been recognised
by one of the merchants with whom he had
formerly done business in the smuggling
line. In addition to the fact that the season
was not at that particular time of the year, a
great dulness and depression had come over all
sorts of public entertainments after the occupation of Edinburgh by the hostile army. The
newspapers, the *Courant* and *Caledonian Mercury*,
were filled with lengthy accounts of the progress
of the Prince's troops, and with equally verbose
(and, no doubt, untrustworthy) particulars of
what was doing in London. However, among
the more reputable amusements that Scott
assisted at, was a " Concert of Instrumental and
Vocal Musick, after which will be given *gratis* a
tragedy, with entertainments between the acts,
by M. Fromart and Madame Dumont, and
dancing by Mistress Thomson."

The Theatre, or " Concert Hall" as it was
called, in order to evade the terms of the Act of
1737, was the Taylors' Hall in the Cowgate.

So there, by five o'clock in the afternoon, Scott and his acquaintance Conway, who was always ready to join in with parties of pleasure, wended their way up the Cowgate, and entering the stage door in Scott's Close, paid each his half-crown for the right to sit on a plain wooden bench without any back. "The Concert of Instrumental and Vocal Musick" was of course a mere device to ride through the Act of Parliament already mentioned; but it was only through having recourse to such tricks that it was possible to present plays in Edinburgh prior to the granting of the Royal Letters Patent in 1767. The audience did not gather until well on to half-past six, at which time it was understood the tragedy would be "given gratis." Just as the curtain was going to be drawn for this purpose a half tipsy young gentleman stood up in the pit and ordered the "fiddlers" to play "God save the King." Almost immediately there was a counter demand for "You're welcome Charles Stuart." Partisans of both sides now rose from their seats and clamoured with more zeal than sense for their party's tune, until the musicians, suiting their own inclinations, struck up the Jacobite melody with all the power they could. This was the signal for a regular set to between the two parties, and while the majority of the combatants were making free with each other's heads, a few occupied themselves with smashing the fiddles to pieces and chasing the players thereof from their position. A few even mounted the stage, and were busy slashing the scenes with their swords, when a new cause of excitement was added in a shower of missiles—candles, speldrens, pieces of wood, etc.—that came from the gallery above.

While all this was going on our two friends could not, if they had tried, have sat still. In sheer self-defence they had to draw, and were immediately occupied in hand to hand encounters with chance opponents; but whether Royalists or Jacobites it was impossible to say. Scott had but little difficulty in not only holding his own, but in securing a place in a corner of comparative safety, for the chief danger now lay in the chance of being hit by heavy missiles from above; whole benches occasionally making their appearance in mid air, to come crashing down with tremendous force into the pit below. Just as he had gained this harbour he noticed his friend badly set upon by two rough-looking men, who wielded heavy sticks.

Scott was no coward, and in a twinkling had one of these sprawling on the floor; then gaining his friend's side he made as short work of the second, seized Conway in a convincing grasp, and half dragged, half carried him outside the building. Nor were they a moment too soon; for just as they gained the main street, the town guard appeared, who, entering the theatre, arrested several of the disturbers of the peace, and had the place cleared and closed up.

Before this was accomplished let us cast our eyes into another part of the building, namely, the stage: the manager running distractedly about, the female performers screaming, and the male ditto swearing; presently, as already said, several bold rioters climbed over the spikes, that then occupied the position of the footlights of the present day, and proceeded to make havoc with the scenes. This liberty the actors who had a share in the concern could ill brook, and at once drew to defend their property. While this was going on a stout gentleman with exceptionally fat legs might have been seen climbing over the Rubicon between pit and stage, and having gained the desired region, instead of making senseless war upon canvas presentments, turned to the side of the stage, and after the lapse of only a few moments, again came into sight, half dragging, half carrying the form of a young girl who was vigorously attempting to gain her freedom.

"Fut for wull she no come at all ? She wull be more kind to her whateffer ; if she wull only come and not make so many screams surely." This Highland eloquence, however, was unavailing, and the young lady screamed more loudly than before for help.

To gain the outer door this gentleman and his captive had to cross from one wing to the other,and in doing so the cries of the young lady happened to attract the attention of a tall gentleman, of a commanding aspect, who was muffled up in a thick cloak, under the folds of which could be easily seen locks of dark red hair, and eyes of startling blackness. In a moment this individual barred the exit, and demanded that the girl should be set free. He of the stout limbs looked at the individual who thus disputed his passage, and for a moment or two seemed as if struck dumb with astonishment. Contrary to all laws of the fitness of things, his legs trembled beneath him, and sinking with great difficulty on one

knee, exclaimed with manifest contrition in his
tones, "If your Highness wulls it—she maun
do her Highness' bidding, whateffer, surely!"

Freed from his grasp, the girl made one spring
to put herself under the protection of the stranger,
who now had in reality become her saviour for the
time, and promptly fainted away in that gentleman's arms. He lifted her up, and taking her outside the building, thought it would be wisest and
best to carry her direct to his own lodgings, which,
indeed, were within a stone's throw. Arrived
there, somewhat out of breath at having to carry
his burden up four flights of steps, he placed the
still insensible girl in the keeping of his landlady, a good sensible woman, to whom he
rapidly told as much of his tale as he deemed
necessary. But her surprise at the narration
was as nothing to his when Mistress Rutherford,
for such was her name, stooping down to loosen
the girl's clothes, recognised her face, and with
a cry of combined joy and horror, exclaimed,
"Shair as deeth, if it's no Katie—Katie Tamson, and rigget oot in siccan a fashion. Losh!
peety me, what wud her mither, honest, dacent
wumman, say if she saw her noo!"

"Then you know the girl, Mistress Rutherford ?" queried Mason, beginning to see some light breaking through the problem he had been trying to solve for so long.

"Ken her! the hussy, I didna' ken she was after sic deevil's pranks as to join the play-actor fouk."

"But her mother ?" impatiently again queried Mason.

"Ay, her mither, puir dacent wumman, she'll be in an awfu' way when she hears o' this."

"Does she live here in Edinburgh ?"

"Na, na, she bides awa' at Tranent."

Mason did not wait to hear more. He had seen Scott in the theatre as he stood upon the stage, which he had newly entered as the disturbance began ; of that he felt certain. Then this girl's cries attracted his notice. That she was being abducted was certain : but by whom ? who was the mysterious being who addressed him as "Your Highness," and for whom could he have been mistaken ?

Then, that this girl should turn out to be the identical person that Scott ran off with ! The whole matter was strange in the extreme, and the Custom House officer, after satisfying himself that there was now no one who had taken part in the riot still about the theatre, walked rapidly to and fro in the wide expanse of the Grassmarket, which was at one moment brilliantly lit up by the rays of the moon, and at another thrown into comparative darkness as a black cloud would scurry across her disc. His thoughts resembled the chequered nature of the night, dark at one moment with plottings and schemes, and, at another, as bright as the moonlight itself, when a vision of two lovely eyes recurred to his memory, along with the recollection of a form of surpassing grace that had but lately reposed within his arms.

CHAPTER VIII.

LITTLE sleep visited the eyes of Mason that night, and he was astir at an earlier hour than usual.

The first thing he did was to interview Mistress Rutherford, and from her he obtained, along with much irrelevant matter, the following particulars. By her statement, it appeared that Lucky Thomson had an aunt living in Edinburgh, to whom there came Kate, some six weeks before, stating that her mother wished her to remain with her aunt until the country was in a less disturbed condition, and more especially that the inn at Tranent had been so seriously damaged, in the manner already recorded, as to be scarcely habitable. Mistress Rutherford further said that she had only a very slight acquaintance with Kate's grand-aunt, but in former years had met Lucky Thomson in that lady's house on one or two occasions. Kate's mother she knew to be a hard-working woman, and certainly, to the best of her belief, in no way connected with the smuggling business. Kate, she had always heard, was a quiet, good girl, helping her mother in the business, and how she had "come to be given over to Satan and his deeds of darkness," as she termed all matters in the slightest way connected with the theatre, she could not understand. She meant to wash her hands of the whole affair as quickly as possible, and her intention was to return the girl to her grandaunt's without a moment's delay.

This latter resolve did not suit Mason's plans in the least, so he lost no time in summoning to his aid the full power of that exceptional influence he possessed at all times, of being able to persuade women, it mattered not of what age or temperament, to act in the directly contrary manner to what they themselves had previously resolved upon. With Mistress Rutherford he had but little trouble, and after making her promise to do nothing, at any rate until he returned, he proceeded, in the first place, to re-dress himself with particular care, and, as the chimes of St Giles chimed

out their merry peal of noon, Mason might
have been observed wending his way through
several of the narrow closes piled together so
thickly on either side of the High Street, until
he halted four stories up at a massive oak door,
admittance by which could only be obtained,
in the first place, by making use of the
then extensively used tirl-pin, which for cen-
turies served our ancestors both for bell and
knocker.

It was here that Kate's grand-aunt lived, and
presently, in response to several vigorous appli-
cations of the tirl-pin, the door was opened about
three inches by an ill-clad, bare-footed, and red-
headed child, who, without apparently comprehending what Mason said to her, suddenly
slammed to the door, leaving him standing for
about five minutes in nearly total darkness on
the stair-head. At last the door re-opened, and
with a scared expression of mistrust and fear on
her excessively dirty face, the urchin bade him
" Come ben."

Although Mason had no difficulty in persuad-
ing women of ordinary force of character to
adopt his ways of thinking, and doing what he
wished, the grand-aunt, whom he now con-

fronted, he soon found to be a person of quite a different calibre, and one of an originality and character entirely her own.

Although over sixty years of age, this somewhat matured dame still aped the dress and appearance of a girl. She wore high-heeled French shoes, a high bodice, and a large hoop to her dress. Her complexion was a work of art, and her hair a mystery. About her person there was, however, that unmistakable and disagreeable air of untidiness, which is easily enough recognised in effect, but by most so difficult to properly define. The same general slovenliness was also very marked in the appointment and arrangement of the room into which Mason now found himself ushered by the red-headed maid-of-all-work. As he entered, her visitor made a profound bow to the lady, while she, rising from a most uncomfortable high-backed chair, described a little semi-circle with her feet, and having by means of this evolution gathered her skirts into the proper position, she slowly descended, as it appeared, into them. The effect produced to the eye was, that her hooped dress being full of air, not only did not flatten, but positively seemed to rise up all round her body, which disappeared,

until only her head, ornamented with an absurd
crown-piece of feathers, alone remained above
the balloon-like basis of the structure.   In rising
the process was reversed, and then the lady, in a
simpering tone, requested the gentleman to do
her the honour to be seated.   He did her·the
honour, and then without any preface commenced, in his own peculiar but generally effec-
tive manner, a process of cross-examination.

  " I have done myself the honour of calling
upon you, madam, at the request of your niece,
Mistress Thomson, of Tranent, whom, I am
happy to say, I left only a few days ago in
excellent health."

  All that this statement drew from the lady
was a deeply drawn sigh and a throwing of her
eyes up to the ceiling, her hands in the mean time
mechanically manipulating a small snuff-box,
the contents of which she divided in almost
equal parts up her nose and down the front of
her dress.

  " I trust, madam, that you are in good health,
and also your grand-niece, whom her mother
directed me to inquire after particularly."

  This rema̅k had the effect of bringing the eyes
down from their heavenly contemplation in double

quick time, to be levelled with a quick searching glance directed towards her visitor. This
woman then, thought Mason, knows that Kate
left without her mother's permission, and knows
I must be telling a lie. She merely remarked—

"I am vera much obleeged for your call, Maister
—eh?"

"Scott—Will. Scott," Mason interjected.

"Maister Scott, I'm glad ma gran'-niece and
mysel' are in gude health; and will ye be seein'
ma niece again soon?"

"That I am not sure of; it will depend on
circumstances."

A pause here succeeded. He had watched
her with the closest scrutiny, but had detected
not the slightest movement of astonishment or
surprise when he gave the name of Scott.

Either she is most uncommonly cunning, or
she does not really know this man 'Scott,
thought Mason. Both felt the pause awkward;
but at last he remarked—

"I had the pleasure of being at the concert last
evening, and I noticed on the bills that a Mistress
Thomson was to appear. I presume she is no
connection of yours?"

"What way?"

"Well, of course; that is, I do not very well know, but at any rate I knew it could not be your grand-niece."

"Did ye see her dancin'?"

"No; did you not hear that there was a disturbance, a perfect riot, and the performance was stopped, and in fact—well, I did feel a little alarmed in case this young lady might be your niece, the name, you see, being the same."

"Oh yes; I ken aboot the riot. I was there!"

"You were!" Mason exclaimed in genuine astonishment.

"Ay; I saw you there tae, and I want to ken what ye mean tae tell yer freend, as ye ca' her, Mistress Thomson, at Tranent, ma niece, what ye did wi' her dochter, ma grand-niece, last nicht!"

Had one great convulsion of nature engulfed, not only the room and the house in which he was seated, but the close, and indeed the whole town of Edinburgh into the bargain, Mason would not have been more thoroughly taken aback than he was by this thunderbolt. He was struck absolutely dumb, and although the lady of gorgeous attire remained motionless sitting opposite him, it seemed to his staring eyes that she grew

gradually into double her size, then double that
again, until the entire room seemed filled with
her presence. How long he might have sat
thus, or indeed how long he did sit, he
could not say, but his trance-like condition
was suddenly disturbed by the entrance of the
aforementioned servant girl, or at least that
portion of her which was crowned by so fine a
crop of almost vermilion hair. Without waiting a second she announced, " It's the gentleman,
mum."

" What gentleman, girl ? "

" Him as says he cam aboot arrestin' the man
as took Mistress Kate."

" Weel, show him intil the breakfast parlour,
and ask him tae bide a few meenits, as I'm particularly engaged."

The head disappeared, a heavy foot was heard
in the passage, and then another door " ben " the
house closed, and all was silence. At last the
lady, in the coolest tone imaginable, inquired,
" Weel, Maister Scott, what am I tae say tae this
gentleman ? " Mason now found the use of his
tongue.

" Madam," he cried, springing from his seat in
a state of uncontrollable excitement, " It's all a

mistake. I can assure you, upon my honour as a gentleman, that it was not I, but a great big hulking fellow, that was trying to carry off your niece; I interfered and saved her, and indeed, that was what I came to tell you about this morning; but, upon my soul, I was not sure whether she was your grand-niece or some one else altogether. She is perfectly safe now in the keeping of my landlady, on the word of an officer and gentleman. I can prove I have never set eyes on the girl since I rescued her last evening."

He paused for want of breath, and she took advantage of the interval to remark—

"Am I also tae lippen tae the messages ye brocht me frae ma niece in Tranent?"

"No, no; I can assure you the whole thing is a mistake. I came here to tell you that she had run away without her mother's knowledge. I cannot explain the circumstances fully just now, but accept my word, and I swear I will make good every word I have said. Come with me just now, and I will prove it."

"Sir," said the dame, "I hae nae desire tae be dootin'yer word. Ye're a gentleman, I ken, and ye will behave as yin, baith tae the young leddy and tae mysel'. You will excuse the liberties I ha'e ta'en wi' ye, but yin has tae be carefu';" making which somewhat ambiguous speech, Mistress Irvine again rose from her chair, and went through the elaborate curtsey which has been described. More and more bewildered, Mason gazed upon her until his two eyes almost started from their sockets, and then an idea flashed through his head, Was the woman raving mad? Surely not, else why the gentleman in the next apartment?

"I see," resumed the lady, when she had emerged from her balloon, "that yer Highness doesna want tae be fashed wi' roondaboot ways o' putting it. It was Sir Michael M'Innes that telt me whae yer Highness was."

"Sir Michael M'Innes?" interrupted Mason.

"Sir Michael M'Innes, yer Highness, and a loyal nobleman he is tae gie up tae your Highness what he had set his heart upon for sae lang; but I dou'tna yer Highness will reward him when yer Highness enjoys yer ain again."

"My good woman, what the—"

But his exclamation was cut short by the lady seizing Mason by the hand, and after kissing that extremity of his body in the most respectful manner, she continued, "But yer Highness

maun mak' haste. I had gi'en word tae the
toun guard last nicht, afore Sir Michael could
tell me whae yer Highness was. Dinna be in the
least alarmed; I'll say it was a' a mistake, that
ma niece had gane awa' wi' a freend, and that
she has come hame again."

The whole truth now flashed across Mason's
mind. He had before this been told that he
bore a striking resemblance to Prince Charles.
Thus Sir Michael M'Innes, whom he had heard
was one of the leaders of the rebels, had
mistaken him in the dim light of the Theatre,
but still he could not comprehend the presence
of that gentleman there at all. He saw one
thing, however, clearly. To escape from the
present predicament, his only chance lay in ac-
cepting the high dignity that had been bestowed
upon him without his choosing.

"Tell me one thing, my good woman," he said,
with an air of superior authority he knew so
well how to assume; "tell me in what way
Sir Michael became acquainted with this girl?"

"Weel, I dinna mind tellin' yer Highness
onything, noo I ken ye are His Highness. It
was this way. He ran awa' wi' her, yer
Highness, frae her mother's house, the day o'

the battle at Prestonpans. When he got tae the camp he fand it wouldna be possible tae keep her there, so he sent her on under a guard tae ma house, alang wi' a very dacent ceevil present tae mysel'. The lassie was delighted tae come tae Edinburgh, and made me promise no tae tell her mither; so Sir Michael he never could wun frae the army till yesterday, and when he called I was surprised tae see that the lassie had ta'en quite a dislike tae him, and wouldna speak tae him; so says I tae him, after she's done at the concert, just you keep yer eye open and awa wi' her. Then besides, there wouldna be ony blame restin' on me if she was ta'en aff in that way. Of course I ken yer Highness will keep ma secret, for I am a dacent woman, wi' a character to keep up, and neighbours will speak ye ken."

"But how was it she came to be at the concert at all?"

"Weel, ye see, yer Highness, I am vera fond o' the play-acting mysel', and whiles the actors come tae ma house, an' she just took it intil her heid, and I didna think it wad dae ony harm, an' of course yer Highness will no forget his servant."

"No, no, of course not, let me out," were

all the words Mason could articulate, and thankful indeed he was to find himself once more in the open air. He had seen many strange sights and had been mixed up in many a curious adventure, but never before in all his experience had he met with anything half so loathsome as this wicked old betrayer of her own flesh and blood, nor for the matter of that had he ever been so completely put in a corner as he had been that morning, nor come out of a scrape so neatly, just at the moment when he imagined he had been completely caught.

In a state bordering almost on stupor he walked smartly along for a considerable distance down the High Street, through the Nether Bow, and on past the Canongate Tolbooth, until he arrived in full view of Holyrood. At this point he was quickly brought to his senses, by seeing on the opposite side of the street the party with the fat legs, whom he now recognised as Sir Michael M'Innes. Fortunately this bold warrior did not notice Mason The chances of him doing so, however, at any moment, were by no means remote, and Mason fully appreciated the folly of exposing himself in the meantime to the possibility of arrest. With-

out question, the old hag grand-aunt would soon
discover that he was not "His Highness" after
all. So would Sir Michael, although that
worthy's wrath was of little moment to him.
But the grand-aunt could make it very uncomfortable for him seeing she had, as it were,
the legal control of Kate, whom, as a matter
of fact, he was detaining from her legal guardian.
That was the difficulty, after all, and what he had
to do to prevent any further trouble to himself, was
simply to send the girl home to Mistress Irvine,
and not bother his head about the matter for
another minute. Clearly the adventure had had
no connection with Scott of any kind whatever,
and Lucky Thomson had in some way or other
unaccountably blundered, or lied, in saying that
the smuggler had run away with the girl. But
would he give her up to her aged relative? No!
a thousand times no! Not if he could prevent it;
and as he turned his steps towards Mrs Rutherford's elevated abode, the picture of that grace-
ful figure clinging to him the night before, filled
his mind with a glow of passion that was too
strong for him to fully comprehend or grasp the
meaning of, as yet.

CHAPTER IX.

WHEN Mason arrived at his lodgings he found Mistress Rutherford waiting for him, with an expression of countenance one would expect a woman of her stamp to assume when she has something at once important and disagreeable to communicate, and which she has been hoarding up in her mind for a long time. In reply to his inquiry as to " how the young lady did," Mistress Rutherford immediately seated herself, an action that always denoted great mental excitement on her part when it was done in the presence of any of her lodgers. Laying her extensive hands on her proportionately extensive lap, she proceeded to " twirl " her thumbs three turns one way, and back again the same number of times the other way, with wonderful regularity considering the extreme agitation of mind under which she seemed to be labouring. Mason was not long in learning from her that her charge had by no

means comported herself to his landlady's liking.
Instead of showing the contrite heart and dejected
manner expected of her, she had amused herself
by singing and dancing about the house all day.
Such levity the matron could not tolerate, and
after reciting a whole catalogue of similar griev-
ous sins, the worthy woman concluded by saying,
that she "was glad Maister Mason had come
baek, so the baggage micht be sent hame." As
for herself, "she washed her hands of her, and
only prayed that a judgment might not be sent
to her for harbouring siccan a backslider." After a
while came her lodger's turn to speak, and while
taking good care not to tell his landlady any more
than was necessary to his purpose, he informed
her that Kate's grand-aunt was a wicked, worthless woman, who had not only persuaded Kate to
go on the stage, but had actually connived at her
attempted abduction the previous night, for
the sake of gain, and that it would be but a
Christian duty and charity to succour and pro-
tect the girl until such time as he could see
his way to take her back to her mother at
Tranent. Beneath much starchiness of manner,
Mistress Rutherford had a good simple heart
hidden away somewhere underneath the surface,

and Mason's story served to set it beating in quite a motherly fashion; and when he multiplied the dangers to the girl, that would attend her restoration to the grand-aunt, she visibly began to relent towards Kate, and finally agreed that she might remain under her protection for the present. This end accomplished, the worthy gauger requested Mistress Rutherford to bring Kate " ben," remarking that she had better stay in the room during the interview. This remark at once brought her back to her normal stiffness of manner, and she quickly replied—

" Dae ye suppose for a meenit I'd leave ye yer twa sels th'gether? no likely, my braw callant!"

If the girl's loveliness had made an impression on the heart of the Custom House officer the previous night, when after all he had had but little opportunity of seeing her, it now sent a thrill of admiration and pleasure through his heart, as he beheld her in all her simple beauty, standing before him in broad daylight, and regarding him with a look of unaffected gratitude. For a moment, and for one of the first times in his life, Mason felt so confused as not to know what to say; Mistress Rutherford quickly broke the spell by informing Kate that Mason wished to give her "a good talking to" about her singing and dancing, and other wicked ways of going on, and she hoped she would listen to what he had to say, as he, Maister Mason, was a good man, and would give her good advice.

All this, of course, was exactly the reverse of what Mason would have wished to be said, for it put him entirely in the light of a stern task-master, and would very likely prevent the girl from forming a favourable opinion of him. There is no doubt that it did tend to prejudice her mind against her deliverer of the previous evening, who speedily found difficulty in extracting anything more than monosyllables from her in the way of replies. All trace of gratitude left her face, and in its place something more of the nature of dogged determination showed itself, all tending to confirm Mistress Rutherford in her conviction that the baggage was no good, and the sooner she could be packed off to Tranent the better. Mason reasoned with the young girl, and pointed out to her, that until she could be restored to her mother Mistress Rutherford had kindly consented to take charge of her, "unless, indeed," he added, "you wish to return to your grand-aunt, in which case, of course, you must just go your own ways."

"No," she replied, "I hate my aunt;" an expression of opinion that shocked the landlady, and drew from Mason the query, "Why it was she hated the old lady?"

"Because she wanted me to do things I didn't like."

In an ordinary way such a reason would scarcely have satisfied Mason, whose sense of duty was very strong. It is the weakness of human nature to dislike people who want to make you do what you do not want, and it is certainly very common for youth to rebel in this way against the course of duty that is laid down for them by their elders. In Kate's case, however, Mason knew that rebellion very probably meant trying to go right against the wishes of the dreadful grand-aunt, whose sense of decency and morality seemed to be based on a subsoil of vice and folly.

"But," queried Mason, "you would like to return to your mother?"

"No; that is, I dinna like the ways down there. It is horrid. Drunken farmers and ministers sit, nicht after nicht, ca'ing me what they think

are bonny names, till they get ower drunk to ca'
me onything."

Speaking about ministers in such a fashion was
more than Mistress Rutherford could patiently
put up with, so she abruptly terminated the interview by hurrying Kate out of the room, with
a running accompaniment of words somewhat to
the effect that no good could come of a baggage
that talked so about sacred things.

Mason was but ill-pleased at the result of the
interview, and as he strode, at a rapid pace, down
the High Street soon after, he revolved within
his mind the various features of Kate's curious
escapade, and the more he turned them over the
more difficult did he find it to make up his mind
as to what he should do.

"Bah," at length he exclaimed half aloud, "why
on earth need I bother or give the chit another
thought? What is she to me? Far better take
her off to her mother at once, and then I am
done with the whole affair!"

Forcing his thoughts into this train of reasoning, and in the midst of his rapid walk, he suddenly paused, recollecting that he was walking
in exactly the contrary direction to that he had
intended; so, muttering something remarkably

like a curse at his own stupidity, he turned and
retraced his steps, still finding fresh arguments
in his mind in favour of sending Kate home
without any delay. So he walked on until he
reached the West Port, just outside of which,
in Portsburgh, he had some business to transact.
Having finished, and without really any definite
object, he strolled leisurely in a westward direction,
until in a few minutes he was entirely away from
the houses, and apparently alone on the narrow
road that then was the only connection between
the capital and the industrious and thriving town
of Glasgow. Gaining some higher ground, near
where now is the busy centre of traffic called
Tollcross, but which then was little better
than waste land, thickly covered with bushes,
and in reality forming the northern extremity
of the Burgh moor, Mason was startled by seeing seated, on a very old and dilapidated seat at
the side of the road, no other than the very Kate
Thomson about whom he had been so greatly
preoccupied during the last twenty-four hours.
She was seated with her back towards him, and
his first impulse was to turn and leave her.
That intention scarcely had time to become for-
mulated in his mind, when it was quickly altered

into a determination to give her a good lecture
on the imprudence of straying so far from the
town, after which he would escort her back to Mrs
Rutherford's, preparatory to her return home on
the morrow.

With this intention in his mind, and a remarkably wise sentence on the tip of his tongue, with
which to open the proceedings, he advanced, but,
just as his lips parted with the object mentioned,
Kate turned suddenly, and observing Mason
jumped up, a deep flush overspreading her face,
and, without the slightest constraint, cried
out—

"Oh! Mr Mason, I'm sae glad you've come.
Is'nt it bonny here? and I was sae chokit up in
that horrid house."

"Yes," he replied, "but how did you find your
way here? Are you not frightened?"

"Frichtened, no! I asked Mrs Rutherford if
I micht go out a walk, and she said I micht if
I didna go far; just tae here, and is'nt it
bonny?"

She had sat down again, and Mason, without
thinking at all what he was doing, and entirely
forgetting the resolve he had so recently made,
sat down beside the young girl, and before he

was aware of it was talking to her as pleasantly
and freely as if he had known her for years.

She with her quick woman's wit easily saw
her mistake of the morning, in imagining Mason
to be the sort of individual sketched by Mistress
Rutherford, and finding him frank and free in
his conversation prattled away without heeding
very much what she said. Without the smallest
embarrassment she related her elopement with
M'Innes, and Mason easily divined that the
whole thing on her part was a mere girlish
freak, gone into without a thought of the consequences, which, of course, might have been
very different. That they had not, was no fault
of the bald-headed old villain, who with the con-
nivance of her grand-aunt had attempted her
abduction in the concert hall; but Kate seemed to
look upon the whole affair, now that the danger
was past, as a joke. After chatting so for an hour,
which seemed to Mason the shortest he had
ever spent, he ventured to hint that she would
require to return home at an early date, an
intimation that at once checked the flow of her
tongue, and caused her to assume a look of
annoyance.

"You do not like the life there," he said,

"but remember it is your duty; and besides,
you must learn to honour your father and
your mother. Duty is not always agreeable,
but it is best in the long run. I have
often most disagreeable duties to perform, but
it would be more disagreeable still to me if I
shirked them. You can't go back to your grand-
aunt, and you can't stay with me."

"Oh, why not ?" she cried, without thinking
for a moment what she was saying; but the
next moment she had realised what a mistake
she had made, the blushes mounted to her face,
and then the tears started to her eyes. She
cried, "Oh, I am a puir, miserable lassie, and I
dinna ken what tae dae."

Poor Mason felt an amount of sympathy for
the beautiful girl that for the moment deprived
him of the power of speech. A sudden impulse
seized hold of him, and in a moment, he
could never say how, Kate was clasped in his
arms, and in passionate terms he conjured her
to allow him to be her protector, and not, if he
was able to prevent them, would tears ever
again dim those eyes of hers. She listened to
all he had to say with simple faith, and so here
were these two building up for themselves

castles in the air which would affect their whole
lives for weal or for woe; they might be the
entrance to paradise, but much more likely
would topple over upon their builders' heads,
crushing, or at least overwhelming, them both
in the downfall.

While walking home **Mason** easily persuaded
Kate to adopt a different manner towards Mistress
Rutherford, who looked upon anything in the
shape of levity as belonging to the evil one, and
it was wonderful, even to herself, to find how
easy the task became when it was prompted by
the most potent of all feelings, love. Such is
the power of that mysterious **factor** in human
affairs. Those who are inspired by its glorious
influence can **see** clearly the problems of life,
and what has formerly seemed irksome and
vexatious becomes suddenly transformed into a
pleasing duty.

It must not be supposed, however, that **Kate**
was the least conscious that she was in love; and
far less was Mason for the matter of that. Love
is like unto an insidious disease, that engrafts
itself upon the heart of man and woman with
so soothing and pleasing a touch, that before
its presence is properly discovered it has

already grown to be a strong and flourishing stem.

Mason had never felt himself so completely in a dilemma before in his life. His duty, as such a matter is estimated by the world and its unwritten laws of conduct, clearly pointed to the necessity of him sending Kate back to her mother. Duty of another kind, however, pointed in a different direction, and as inclination very strongly supported the latter, it is not difficult to foresee which of the two eventually won the day.

So back to Mistress Rutherford they came, where that virtuous lady, after a terrible row delivered at Kate for staying out so long, was eventually greatly mollified by a circumstantial and apparently sincere statement of regret for past backslidings, and a binding promise of amendment in the future from Kate.

CHAPTER X.

SEVERAL days passed over, and although not
neglecting the smallest portion of his work, and
above all things keeping a sharp lookout for Scott,
Mason contrived to spend many hours with
Mistress Rutherford and Kate, the latter of
whom, however, he did not have an opportunity
of again seeing alone.

As was to be expected, Mistress Irvine
waited somewhat impatiently for a substantial
token of gratitude from "His Highness," and
felt considerably aggrieved, as day after day
passed and no word or present came to reward
her for her devotion to his royal person. A
considerable portion of her afternoons were
devoted to earnest conversation with Sir Michael
M'Innes, whose interest in herself and the
recent affair with Kate she took care to
stimulate from time to time, by narrating an
imaginary conversation she had had with "His

Highness," in which she related that that royal
individual had specially commended his, Sir
Michael's loyalty, hinting that only the highest
honours would eventually suffice to express
his royal thanks when "the King enjoyed
his own again."

Notwithstanding all this and his own recollection of beholding the Prince with his own
eyes, Sir Michael was very much puzzled at
the fact of Charles being in Edinburgh at all.

He himself had no business to be there;
but so madly in love was he, that he had
even risked deserting the army, while it lay at
Peebles, in order to see the girl he had taken from
the Tranent Inn, and if possible get possession of
her person.   Under these circumstances, to find
his Royal master in full possession as it were,
was, to say the least of it, extremely annoying.

Being physically of a nature not over-well
formed for active exercise, his residence in the
capital was eminently more to his taste than
marching over wild moors and mosses and sleeping in the open, as he should have been compelled to do had he remained with the army;
an additional attraction lay in Mistress Irvine's
acquaintance with the play-actors, who met fre-

quently in her house, so his time passed agreeably enough during the days he waited for the expected token of gratitude from his royal master.

One afternoon, while he and the old lady were sitting discussing various matters of little moment, a message was brought Sir Michael which had been sent, post from the camp, and which informed him that the Prince, in great displeasure at his withdrawal from the army, had deprived him of his command, and would refuse to receive him even if he presented himself to crave his royal pardon. This missive, although written by Secretary Murray, was signed Charles P. in the royal handwriting.

M'Innes jumped from his seat, and he swore in English (bad in two respects) and he swore in Gaelic, and the latter sounded like the noise made by bagpipes when the piper is full of wrath, and seeks to announce his passion through the medium of music. He swore at himself, and he swore at Mistress Irvine, and he swore at everybody; but she, being the only person within the lash of his tongue, naturally got the most of it.

It was not until Sir Michael had finally

I

sworn himself out at the door, and left a parting
malediction on the red head of the barefooted
urchin who opened it to him, that Mistress Irvine
began to suspect that she had, in some way or
another, been duped. She recalled all that the
supposed Prince had said to her, and the more
she thought over it the more she felt certain of
it, especially when she recollected that the name
" His Highness " had given her was the same as
one Kate had mentioned to her as being present
when the floor fell in at Tranent. Kate's
mother had informed her daughter of the fact
of Scott's presence among the Highlanders,
and now the suspicion came into Mistress Irvine's
mind, that Kate had planned the whole thing be-
forehand with this very man. The running away
with M'Innes, so as to avert suspicion, and all
the rest of it, and her rage, when she thought
of the handsome sum of money M'Innes had
promised her, and the still more magnificent
present she had expected to receive from her
supposed Prince, was of an intensity suitable to
the black wickedness of her unhealthy mind.

Her first impulse was to put the authorities
on the track of this man Scott, but that would
be a matter that required caution in the doing,

seeing that she had already informed them that
her grand-niece had come home safely in company with a friend. She finally resolved to
wait a little and see what would happen.
M'Innes might be mistaken in the second
instance instead of the first; in other words,
the wish being father to the thought, it might
have been the Prince after all.

Several days passed by without anything
important happening, until one forenoon, as
Scott was passing up one of the closes in the
compact region of houses between the Parliament Hall and the Cowgate, he was suddenly
confronted by a couple of the town guard, armed
and evidently ready for work. At last he had
been tracked, but not caught; not yet, while
he had legs with which to run. His Border
blood was up in a moment; but fighting under
the circumstances being preposterous, he turned
on his heel and sped down the close at a pace
that left his would-be captors far behind. They,
seeing their bird nearly safe away out of their
clutches, raised the cry, "Stop rebel!" "Stop
rebel!" Now it so happened that, just at the
foot of the close, several persons were standing
together, in idle consultation upon the latest

news. One of them happened to have a copy of the *Caledonian Mercury*, which had been issued that morning, and he was busily reading it aloud to the others, when the cry, " Stop rebel!" caught their ears, and looking whence the noise proceeded, they beheld a man making the best use of his legs to escape the two emissaries of the law, the dignity of which was in no danger of being sacrificed by any undue precipitancy in the persons of its representatives. Such a chase was quite to the liking of a gathering of the lower orders, whose love of sport in any form was much in excess of any chance they had of gratifying it. Scott, therefore, would not have been hindered in his headlong course, and probably would have escaped literally " Scot free," had it not so happened that, at the very moment he reached the termination of the close, a lady of respectable age, but dressed with great attention to display, stepped from the Cowgate pavement at right angles to the direction Scott was going, and to within not more than three or four inches from his person. The mouth of the close was not more than six or seven feet wide, and Scott, who had inclined slightly towards one side in order to turn the corner, just escaped running

right against her. As it was, he involuntarily
swerved to the opposite side, and in doing so
slipped his foot and fell with tremendous force
on the causeway. The lady screamed, the
loungers rushed forward, and finally the law
arrived, with dignity at par, but breath very
much below, and to put it shortly Scott was
captured. Now, however, came the curious part
of the thing. A tradesman, with cap and apron,
and his shirt sleeves rolled well up his arms,
who had been one of the loungers at the corner,
entered into conversation with the guard, inquiring, "For what noo may he be taen up?"
"His name," replied the law, "is Wull Scott, an'
he is a maist notorious rebel and thief, forbye
bein' a smuggler, an' a murderer intil the
bargain!"

Before the tradesman, who was evidently
going to speak, could utter a word, the elegantly
dressed female, who had stopped screaming
when she found that nobody took any notice of
her, sprang forward, and cried out with much
energy,. "Wull Scott! that's no Wull Scott, ye
gowks;" which statement was instantly con-
firmed by the tradesman who had spoken before.
"Na, na, ma men; ye've made a mistake this

time. I ken this gentleman weel, he's Maister
Blaikie, an' a guid leeberal gentleman he is
forbye." Of which opinion he felt so confident,
that he bestowed a knowing nod of the head to
his friend the blacksmith, who was standing
with his hands resting one on each hip, looking
wise beyond his station. "Weel-a-weel," remarked the latter person, "if so be the gentleman is a gentleman, and he looks gey an' like
yin, there's nae use haudin him."

This turn of affairs took Scott much more by
surprise than had the former, but already he
had had plenty of time to profit by it.

"I 'm obleeged tae this lady, and you ma guid
freens, for the service ye hae done me; here's
some siller, ma men, tae get a drink wi'!"

Doubtful at first, the "siller"—when does it
not?—dispelled all doubts in the minds of the
law representatives, and Scott *alias* Blaikie
walked forth none the worse for his adventure,
save in his dress, which was considerably torn
and plentifully bedaubed with mud.

Just at this moment, as the friendly tradesman was repeating to the blacksmith his
knowledge of Mr Blaikie's identity, and the
respectable lady of gorgeous attire was inform-

ing the two town-guards that she knew the real
Will. Scott by sight, and, in fact, was entering
upon a most elaborate description of that individual's person; just as this was going on,
the attention of the crowd was again startled by
a loud exclamation from the lady. She pointed
up the close, down which was seen coming a tall
individual of striking appearance, in whom dark
red hair and black eyes were prominent features.
"See," at last she cried, "there is the man ye
want; tak him up, the monster, that's Wull
Scott;" and so on she raved with a vehemence
that was extraordinary, and, no doubt, had
Mason, for it was he, heard what she was saying, or seen who it was making all the noise, he
would very likely have turned tail, as Scott had
so recently done, and reascended the close much
quicker than he had already descended it. He
came on, however, in a state of happy dreaming, need it be said on what subject, and when
within a few yards of the crowd, curiosity as to
what it was gathered together for, led him right
into the middle of it, and so into the clutches of
the now delighted guardians of the peace. No
explanations could avail. It was conceivable
that they might have been guilty of a mistake

once; but not twice. Such a thing was impossible, and here they had a witness by their side, who positively swore to the man's identity. To make quite sure, one of the town-guards appealed to his friend the tradesman, who turned to the blacksmith, and was about to deliver himself of some remark, no doubt of great wisdom, when he was interrupted by a man of large dimensions and rubicund countenance, who, with perfect conviction in his tone, said— "It's maist likely its just him, and ye're best tae mak' sure onyway;" and turning to his neighbour, the smith, he remarked, "It's only a gauger onyway, I ken him for a mean thief, that winna let ony yin keep a gill o' free brandy intil their house." This gentleman, who was addressed as Tam Lancashire by his neighbours, seemed to be an authority, whose word was not to be gainsaid, for without any more ado Mason was marched off in the direction of the Tolbooth. Mistress Irvine, for she it was who had been so forward in stultifying the ends of justice, spoke to Lancashire, with whom she seemed to be on excellent terms, and asked him when again the play-house would be opened, to which that worthy replied, " 'Deed, madam, but

I'm no sure. I do hear-tell of a grand new pro-
ject to big a braw new theatre in the Canongate,
and Maister Ryan is comin' frae London tae dae
it."

Having chatted with Mistress Irvine for some
time, Lancashire turned to the few of the crowd
still remaining, and said, "And now, freends, I
dinna think we can dae better like, than step
up to the 'Cape Club' and hae our meridian."

And they went, for Tam Lancashire, be it
known, combined the profession of acting with
the trade of publican, in the former of which
occupation he acquired fame, and in the latter
fortune.

CHAPTER XI.

AFTER his extraordinary escape from the clutches of the law, Will. Scott made all convenient haste to his tavern, and was busily employed in commemorating the lucky outcome of his adventure in the flowing bowl, when he was joined by his acquaintance Conway. The latter seemed particularly grave in his demeanour, a fact that Scott rallied him upon; for he himself felt uncommonly merry after the romantic results of the morning. It was his nature.

At last, as they sat drinking their wine together, Conway leaned over the table, and, with much earnestness of manner, spoke as follows—

"If you will permit me my friend, to speak to you about your affairs, I should be very glad, as I have something to tell you that may be of much importance to you."

Scott bestowed a searching look at his friend

and then said—"I am sure ye're maist kind an' freendly."

"That shall be as it may be," replied Conway. "But, in the first place, I want you to thoroughly understand, that I *am* your friend, and what I am going to tell you, is purely in the way of friendship—and warning."

Scott again eyed Conway carefully, but did not speak.

"Before I go any further," continued the other, "am I to consider that you will receive what I am going to tell you in a friendly spirit?"

"Yes!" at length replied Scott, while at the same moment he extended his hand over the table, and gave Conway's a hearty grip; "I believe ye are ma freend, wi' a' ma soul."

"Now!" said the other, "I will tell you more: why I am your friend, for instance. You saved me from injury, perhaps from being killed, on the night of the concert. Had it not been for you, I do not think I should have been enjoying this excellent claret so well just now. When a man does me a good turn, I never forget it; and you did me a good turn,—I hope I may be able to do you another."

He paused, but, as Scott maintained silence, he merely sipped his wine, and then proceeded.

"I found out the first day I met you that your name was not Blaikie, and also the fact that you had been in the Pretender's army."

Scott started.

"I did not know then, but I do now, who you are, and in fact, all about you. I am a man of the world remember, and as your actions are of no consequence to me, the knowledge shall not go beyond me. I have found you in everything to be a gentleman, and a brave one as well, so I wish to try to help you just now. I may be running some risk myself in doing so; but that doesn't matter. What I have got to tell you is, that you are in danger here, for there are those who are very keen to secure you; and one man there is, who has sworn to have you, dead or alive, and at the present moment I think he is on your track; in fact, he must be, or how else would he have been able to tell the guard about you to-day?"

"Hoo dae ye ken aboot that?" demanded Scott.

"Never mind about that just now, my friend. This man—"

"I ken him," interrupted Scott; "but I hae jinked him twice already, an' I'm no feared o' him. Excuse me for askin'—mind ye, I believe ye are ma freend—but whae are ye yersel? I canna mak ye oot at a'."

"Few people can," replied Conway, with an air of mystery, "but I'm not prepared to tell you exactly who or what I am. To resume, I heard to-day that you had been taken and locked up, and I hastened here to try and learn the truth, and I am pleased to find I was misinformed. But how did you escape? I have not heard that part of the affair yet."

Scott, in considerable glee, then and there related how he had been arrested, when, by some extraordinary chance, he had been immediately set free through the agency of an unknown "grand" lady, and how, in addition, his enemy had afterwards been taken in his place and removed to the Tolbooth.

All this astonished and amused Conway greatly, and served him as well as anything else as a text on which to preach the necessity of Scott at once fleeing the town, or at least getting into a safer hiding-place.

He finished his advice, and then said—

"Now, my friend, we must part. I have endeavoured to repay you in some sort for the debt of gratitude I owe you. Remember, I can do no more for you, the rest you must do for yourself. Goodbye."

And so they parted: the one to ponder and think who this strange man could be, who seemed to know everything; and the other, to wend his way up to the Tolbooth, whither we shall follow him. Having arrived, and when the huge key had turned in the enormous lock to allow him to enter, he found Mason had already been set free, although still in the building. Telling the Custom House officer he wished to speak to him, they were on the point of leaving, in order to find more comfortable quarters in John's tavern opposite, when a stylishly dressed lady, who had just entered, suddenly rushed forward, and pointing to Mason, exclaimed, "That's the man; pit him in irons till he brings me ma grand-niece, wha he stole at the concert."

As might naturally be expected, the warders and turnkey of the prison, as well as Conway himself, stared in undisguised amazement. Mason himself, however, looked confused, while the lady continued to impeach him with no end of crimes.

At last the turnkey, annoyed at her persistency, exclaimed—

" Gang awa' woman, ye're either bletherin' or fou."

But a woman of Mistress Irvine's stamp was not to be so easily put down, and turning from Mason, she proceeded to vent her wrath upon the unlucky official, who had ventured to impute drunkenness to her. Finding, however, that the turnkey was made of impenetrable stuff, she again assailed Mason, not only with her tongue, but with more lasting instruments of torture, to wit, her nails, which, before one of the bystanders could come to his assistance, she had deeply implanted in his face. From this assault she was at length dragged by force, when her nerves having been worked up to too high a state of tension, she immediately collapsed into hysterics.

While the fit lasted, Mason deemed it best to beat a retreat, so, along with his friend Conway, he crossed the High Street, and chose a cosy nook in John's tavern, for a friendly " crack " and bottle. For a good while Mason had to stand a considerable quantity of friendly banter or chaff from his companion on the head of his acquaintanceship with Mistress Irvine, whose character and reputation (or want of both) Conway knew well. At length Mason, having got his companion to be serious for a little, told him his tale. When at last he concluded, by saying, that the girl was still under Mistress Rutherford's charge, Conway's face became serious enough for anything.

"This," he said, "is a much graver matter than I anticipated. Mason, I am afraid you must pack the girl off to her mother."

"But she doesn't want to go back there; the life is one she hates; and then, what would be her reception, after having run away?"

"Tut, tut, man, you speak as if you were madly in love with the girl; and, by Jove, now I come to look at you, my fine fellow—ha, ha, that's how the wind lies, is it?"

"Tush, nonsense, Conway. I do like the girl, that's true; she's both pretty and amiable, but then she would never have a poor devil like me. Why, look at the roving life I must needs lead for the next few years before I get all this smuggling put down."

"Never you fear, my friend. The die has got to be cast. If you are willing to marry the girl—

why, ask her. If she is in the same frame of
mind, then marry her *at once*. If she is not in
the same frame of mind, well, what's the use of
your bringing yourself into trouble for a girl
that does not care for you? Simply pack her
home and be done with the affair. There, you
have the best advice I can give you. If you
succeed, I will be your best man; now, I can't
promise more, and I wager you I'll be the first
to kiss the bride."

"Thank you," said Mason, extending his hand
to his friend, "and your advice is good. I never
think long about things. To think with me is
to do. I will go to my rooms at once and ask
her; do you, my friend, come with me and explain the matter to Mistress Rutherford. I am
more nervous about her than anything else."

"No, no," replied Conway; "I make it a rule
never to interfere in love affairs; besides, you
can do it better by yourself; but before we go,
there is one thing I should like to ask you, and
I trust you will not think me impertinent."

"Certainly not; I am sure you will be actu
ated by true friendship in anything you ask."

"That is so. Now, you have told me this young
lady's history pretty minutely, but one thing you

K

did not mention—remember, I do not wish to cast any reflections on her, or to ask you anything you may not wish to answer; but have you ascertained *why* she ran away with this Sir Michael M'Innes ?"

" To be candid with you, no, I have not; but I do not think Kate knows herself. That no harm came of her foolish action, I admit, was no fault of hers, but still no harm did come of it; her virtue seems to have been watched over by a higher power, with a care and solicitude that it does not usually exercise in the case of young girls who make their first little mistake in life. I am perfectly certain it was a mere girlish freak; that she never considered for a moment what she was doing any more than a child, who, rushing on a newly frozen pond, and is drowned in consequence, reflects before committing the fatal deed the price it will pay to gratify its desire."

" You take, indeed, a broad view of the case."

" No, I take a merciful view; and if men, instead of professing a sham gallantry towards women, while all the time they are carrying on shameful intrigues, would judge them, not by a more or less impossible ideal, but by the *standard of their own lives*, they would have little fault to find, as a rule, on the score of virtue."

"I must say, I never thought of it so; you are quite a philosopher."

"To come to the point, I feel I love this girl, and if she is willing to give me her heart and hand, I care nothing for the past."

"Supposing she gives you the hand without the heart?"

"In that case I will do my best to compel the heart to follow the hand."

"And, by St Andrew, you are the sort of man to do it successfully too; but come, it grows late—this is Friday. The banns must be cried on Sunday, and you married the same day, if possible; let's away."

Let us now return to Tranent for a while, where there was to be seen a pony, saddled, and waiting at the door of the inn, from which presently emerged the mistress thereof, who mounted and rode away in the direction of Edinburgh. There she arrived safely in due course, and dismounted at the door of her aunt's house upon this very Friday evening.

When the two women met it could easily have
been seen, that while they lavished much affection
upon each other, in the way of expressions of
friendship, they nevertheless thoroughly dis-
trusted and hated one another, and were conse-
quently each waiting for the other to begin upon
the real business of the visit. At last the elder
remarked, with an air of total unconcern, " Dae
ye ken that your dochter's here in the toun ? "

" Whaur hae ye seen her ? " queried the
mother, allowing her maternal instinct to get
the better of her prudence.

" Ay, I hae seen her, the baggage, and a fine
kettle o' fish she's been frying for hersel, and a
fine botheration folk's been at, all on account
o' her cantrips ; but I hae done wi' her, I wash
ma hands o' her."

The aunt then related that Kate had come
to her saying that she had been sent, after
which she had run away with a gentleman,
whose name she said, she had been told, was
M'Innes. The last she had seen of her, however, had been with a man called Scott.

The devil can quote Scripture, and so could
Mistress Irvine, when she liked ; and this being,
to her mind, a suitable occasion on which to show

her knowledge of Holy Writ, she interlarded her recital with it pretty freely.

The mother's grief and sorrow was not only excessive, but genuine, and even Mistress Irvine, with heart of stone, felt compelled to sympathise with her. She assured the sorrowing parent that she had done everything to reclaim the wanderer, but that she had been removed, no one knew where, by this villain Scott, who not only was at the bottom of every mischief, but also seemed to be able to walk out of prisons as easily as other people found it to walk into them; and then she told her niece about the incident of that very forenoon.

It was just at the gloaming, and the two women had occasion to sally forth into the street together. Almost the first person they met was no other than Will. Scott, who, never thinking, ran almost against them. In a moment he was in the grasp of Lucky Thomson, who held on to him with a fury almost indescribable. Mistress Irvine, on the other hand, recognising the man who so nearly knocked her to the other side of the Cowgate in the morning, again commenced to explain that it was not Scott. But Lucky Thomson's fury there was no quieting. A crowd speedily collected, and one man of a forward nature, under the impression that the woman must be drunk, dealt her a blow with his stick that stunned her. The crowd, not noticing who had done this, and naturally attributing it to Scott, cried, " Shame! shame!"

Things had an angry look, and for the second time that day, the bold ex-smuggler took to his heels and ran, as he had but seldom run before. The crowd of smart young apprentices and stalwart tradesmen was a different pursuit to try and escape from compared to the two aged and overgrown members of the town-guard in the morning, and for a few moments it seemed hardly possible that he would escape.

Down towards the south, then across the Cowgate and into another close on the opposite side, up towards the Greyfriars, he sped. It suddenly occurred to him that the city gates would be closed, cutting off all reasonable hope of escape; but, just at that moment, he beheld standing right in front of him, an old ragged witch-like hag, who shouted to him with shrill vehemence—

" Intae here, Wull Scott; quick, quick!"

It was an inspiration of a moment to follow

the woman's advice; and into an old low-arched doorway, of great massiveness, he almost leapt, with the result that he found himself rolling at the foot of about six stone steps, leading down from the street into a cellar. He could scarcely have reached the ground, however, when he heard the door slammed and a key turned on the inside. In another moment the woman had grasped him by the hand, crying, "Quick, quick, I can save ye; dinna be feared, follow me."

She retained her hold, and almost dragged him through several apartments that were in total darkness. Long ere she had led him away many steps, the crowd could have been heard at the door, kicking and knocking, but with very little chance of passing its portals, unless they could obtain crowbars and sledge hammers to help them.

The woman, cat-like, could either see in the dark, or else knew her way so minutely, that although Scott was conscious of passing all sorts of obstructions so close that some he actually touched, not one did they hit against during their mysterious progress. At length his guide halted, and feeling against what seemed to be a

stone wall, dripping with soft slime, she opened
a small door, from which there ascended a flight
of stone steps, another door at the top, and Scott
found himself with his companion in the back
room of a low, obscure public house, that he at
once recognised as familiar. It had, indeed,
been well known to him at one time as a house
largely interested in the smuggling trade, and
now he knew why the crone had been able to
bring him by the mysterious dark passage; but
he could by no means guess her motive. He
lifted a crusie and held it up to her face.

"Wha hae we here? ma certie, ye did me a
gude turn that time. I ken yer face an' I
dinna. Wha are ye?"

"Wha I am, or wha I may no be, matters
little to you, Wull Scott. I've met ye twice.
I'll meet ye yince again, an' then fare-
weel!"

"Ay, I mind ye now; ye tried tae dae
me an ill turn at the Cleekim Inn, but that's
wiped oot, here's gold for what ye hae done this
nicht. I'm safe noo, an' I've tae thank
ye!"

"Gold, ay, ay; it may be, but pooch yer
trash an' gang yer ways!"

The firs will roar and bend their heid,
  The stream will swollen be,
Then you and me will meet again,
  When ane o' us maun dee!

The crone rushed from the apartment, never having touched the gold piece that Scott had proffered her, and so astonished was he that he did not even attempt to follow. Who she could be or what her purpose in so opportunely saving him he could not fathom, nor could he get any enlightenment from the landlord of the public house, with whom he afterwards had a long chat. Scott had his suspicions, however, that this worthy knew more than he chose to confess. The "Hole in the Wall"—who has not passed the spot, nearly opposite Greyfriars' Churchyard ?—was where Scott was now hidden. The host was delighted to see him, he said, as he had some goods stored in one of the Wrycht's Houses, at Bruntsfield Links, which he wished conveyed to a town in the west, and who so able or fit to undertake the duty as the notorious smuggler Will. Scott !

At midnight, as the moon was shining brightly upon the placid waters of the South Loch, Scott and his host stole out of the window of famous memory, and skirting the shores of the loch on the left, and the grounds of Heriot's Hospital on the right, made their way towards one in the ancient line of houses, the few fast disappearing remnants of which are looked down upon nowadays by that monument of bad taste in architecture, the Barclay Church.

The promised reward, if he conveyed the goods safely to Glasgow, was handsome, and the necessity of earning more money was made very apparent to Scott by the sight of his much diminished stock of guineas, which, " easy gotten," had been " soon spent; " and even one hundred and fifty years ago, a life of idleness, with pleasure for its watch-word, could not be carried on without considerable charges being incurred.

CHAPTER XII

THERE is no moment in all one's life, that lives so freshly or keeps so sweetly in the mind of man, as that in which he first told his true love his passion. Curiously, it has from quite an early date been frequently utilized by writers in quite a different aspect. "Popping the question," as it is popularly termed, has become in ordinary parlance entirely identified with what is amusing and even absurd or grotesque. We have it so in plays, in novels, and even in poetry, although, of course, in the higher reaches of all these branches of writing we find, on the contrary, pathos, sentiment, and the full beauty of romance infused into the descriptions. Much of the artificial in manner must necessarily often occur, when a man devoured by love, blinded it might be called, gasps out his soul's longing to the object of his adoration, and all the time is unconsciously endeavouring to shape and regu-

late his utterances, as much as his actions, by a
more or less inaccurate acquaintance with what
should be and is usually done on such occasions.
Many a man thinks that success is easier to be
attained by the method than by the matter.

In this way, numbers have in reality failed
through studying the letter, as it were, and not
the spirit. If a woman cares for a man sufficiently to marry him, the method in which he
proposes will be of little consequence, although
no doubt it pleases her more to be asked neatly
and with poetic feeling, than to have an abrupt
" Will you marry me ? " interjected into ordinary
conversation. It is also very flattering to the
man to think that he " popped " in a neat and
appropriate manner ; and, on the principle that
things are just as we make them or esteem them,
man will always prize more highly anything
that he has acquired in what he considers a
smart manner. It is owing to this that many
ingenious gentlemen have, from time to time,
indited certain works of the nature of " The
Complete Lover," and " Courtship, and all about
it."

Such works, along with the " Complete Letter
Writer," and, " How to behave as a Gentleman ;

by a Gentleman," command very much larger
sales and are more extensively studied, than
many other books which, if properly studied,
would be much more conducive to courtship
being properly gone about, than those which
profess to teach the truth, the whole truth, and
nothing but the truth, on the subject.

Men of a more original turn of mind than
the students of such special treatises are, however, not always above taking a hint from
extraneous sources.   There is a beautiful "Popping the question " scene in Robertson's play of
"School,"—indeed, there are two,—which have
both, it is pretty certain, served as models for
hundreds and hundreds of such episodes in real
life.   T. W. Robertson was almost always happy
in such scenes ; but of course there are hundreds
and thousands of writers, who have left equally
pretty pictures, for the admiration and use of
posterity.

"Gently he lifted her delicate hand in his,
and as he gazed at it so fondly, his lips gave
expression to his thoughts, and his whole heart
went out in a few words.   'This hand is too soft,
too tender, too beautiful, to battle with this
rude world; mine are strong and rough enough

to fight for two—let them fight and work for these !' "

Such might be considered a poetical way of doing it; but Mason was more a man of action than of sentiment or of poetical ideas; hence probably his distrust in his own chances in his own case. It is peculiar to lovers to believe, that poetry and romance have more influence with women than honest truthfulness and rough manliness. No doubt there are plenty of women in regard to whom this belief would be well founded; but Kate Thomson, although flighty by nature to some extent, was none of these, and Mason need have had no fear, had he but known better how to read that most difficult of all books, a woman's heart.

The incident that had occurred beyond Portsburgh, when a sudden impulse that he could not account for had made him do what, under any ordinary circumstances, he would not have dreamt of doing, caused him to fear more than he might otherwise have done, that his suit would not be successful. He feared it might even have offended Kate so much, that any feeling of gratitude she had formerly felt towards him would now be completely destroyed. He

could but try his chance however, and so with
that determination he turned his steps towards
home.

Arrived there, his intention was to immediately disclose his proposal to Kate in Mistress
Rutherford's presence. This, in every way, he
considered his best course of action, as it would
lend a feeling of genuineness to his actions, that
would in the future disarm any possible criti-
cism. Further, he argued to himself, it would
altogether remove any lingering desire on the
part of his landlady to get rid of her young
charge, while on Mistress Rutherford's sympathy
and co-operation he, of course, reckoned himself
as sure.

On gaining his rooms, he was at first a little
put out of his calculations, by finding that the
old woman was not at home, and Kate taking
advantage of her absence, was busily engaged in dancing round the room to the music
of her own voice, tuned to a lively dance air.
She stopped suddenly, on perceiving Mason
enter, and with a scarcely distinguishable
apology of some kind or other, was about to
run from the room, when Mason checked her
progress by taking her hand in his and asking

her to sit down, as he "had something to say to her."

Blushing crimson she did as she was bid, and scarcely comprehending her own feelings felt sure, all the same, that something that would greatly affect herself was going to happen; but what it might be she could not even dimly guess.

After asking if Mistress Rutherford would likely be long, and being told by her that the old lady had gone out about half-an-hour before without leaving any word, Mason, who had never let go her hand, said in a voice which required his every effort of will to control—

"Kate; I may call you Kate may I not? I can scarcely tell you, what I was going to say, because, that is, since I first saw you at the concert hall, I have had a very high regard and admiration for you, and I am deeply sorry at the unhappy position you are in, because you don't want to go back to your mother's, and it would never do for you to go to your aunt's!"

She sat with downcast eyes, and her left hand twitched nervously. She was intensely excited, almost frightened; but wherefore she could not have said, if she had tried.

" I know," he resumed, " the difficulty of your position, and I—if you will allow me to be your protector, you need not then return at all— Kate, don't you see?   I know I am not worthy of you; but if you can like me ever so little, I will work for you and make you so happy.   Try, will you !—I love you !"

The words were spoken, the effort was over; she looked into his eyes, and in a moment after they were in one another's arms.

" And do you love me, Kate ?"

" Yes."

" And you will marry me ?"

But there was no audible reply to this.

It was at this moment that the door opened, and before the lovers knew, Mistress Rutherford was standing in their presence.   With arms akimbo, she contemplated the scene, her features assuming meanwhile an expression something different from what would be described as one of Christian charity.

Not leaving hold of Kate's hand, Mason rose from his seat, and holding out his disengaged hand, said—

" Congratulate me, Mistress Rutherford ; I am sure you will be delighted to hear that poor

L

Kate's troubles are over, as she has consented to be——"

But the storm of wrath, that had been rapidly infusing in the old lady's breast, at this moment became too much for her to suppress any longer, and with something very nearly approaching a yell of detestation, she rushed at Kate, and actually had planted her nails suspiciously near to the girl's face, when Mason's quick eye and ready hand arrested her further progress by gripping her firmly by the wrists. Not heeding this interruption in the least, the old lady, deprived of the chance of striking at close quarters, opened the artillery of her tongue with tremendous vehemence. Her words were, of course, more forcible than polite, and continued in one steady torrent, until physical collapse supervened, and hysterical tears came plentifully to her relief.

Mason tried his best to show her how utterly absurd her conduct was; that he intended marrying the girl as soon as he possibly could, and that there was not the slightest reason for such a noise and bother.

Every argument he used only made the old lady more hysterical, until, despairing of getting

her to listen to reason, he finished up his remarks by saying—

"Then, Mistress Rutherford, since you persist
in going on in this utterly absurd manner, I will
leave the house, and I will not return until I come
to take Kate to the minister's to be married."

The idea of leaving the girl with her re-
kindled all the old lady's ire; and flaming up
again, she ordered the " baggage " from her door
that moment. She had better go and drown
herself in the Nor' Loch, or throw herself from
the Salisbury Crags, for she would never come to
any good anyway, that was certain; and a great
deal more in the same strain, until Mason, with
Kate clinging to his arm, shaking with fear, and
the tears streaming from her eyes, left the house,
where the possibility of remaining was simply
absurd.

Their steps led them mechanically to the west,
and after a long walk through Portsburgh into
the country beyond, they were retracing their
way, when Mason recollected that, in a cottage
close by, an old woman lived whom he had
known long before, and who would most likely
afford Kate a safe harbour and refuge till such
time as the minister could tie the knot that

would give him the legal right to undertake the charge of the young girl.

The place was easily found, and with the cordial and delightful hospitality that once characterised the country people of Scotland, but which has, alas! either passed away, or been degraded into a mock article, the aim of which is future gain, Kate was cheerfully admitted, and after a tender leavetaking, Mason betook himself again to the town, where, not caring to face his landlady until that worthy champion of virtue had had time to cool somewhat in her virtuous indignation, he bespoke a room in Fortune's tavern, and spent a wakeful night thinking over the events of the day.

CHAPTER XIII.

HOWEVER gay Mistress Irvine might be through the week, she was punctiliousness itself in the matter of—what was at that time considered—proper Sabbath observance. She had scarcely ever been known to miss a kirk service. The bi-annual Sacramental "Fast" time was observed by her with a rigour that was the envy of her personal acquaintance in the congregation, and last, but not least, the most suspicious among her neighbours admitted that her house was always properly regulated, although there might be other reasons for keeping down one's blinds on the Sabbath besides religion.

In short, she had a splendid record, and was held up by the worthy elders of her kirk as being "a maist saintly wumman; and, although she did dress a bit braw, she was a guid Christian, and aye plankit doun her saxpence intil the kirk ladle o' Sawbaths."

Seemingly these estimable gentry held, that, on the principle that one should not let the left hand know what the right hand doeth, they need not concern themselves with her going to concerts and such like works of the devil; in fact, as they had never of necessity seen her in such places, and had always refrained from asking her if she attended them, they were not supposed to know anything of the matter at all.

Bible in hand and Knox's psalter, Mrs Irvine was one of the first who responded on Sundays to the general invitation to worship rung forth from every steeple, and so it is not surprising to see her issue forth from her stair on the Sabbath following the events recently enacted, accompanied by her niece.

It was to St Giles' that they wended their way, and in that particular portion of it called for so many years the High Kirk, took their seat in the pew wherein Mistress Irvine had a sitting.

It happened to be a particularly warm day for the time of year, and as the pew, owing to Lucky Thomson's portly presence, had one more occupant than it was seated for, the comfort of those inside diminished as the temperature rose.

Even to this day there is a musty smell permeating the air of this historic building on warm days. Considering the number of Scottish kings and their subjects that have been buried underneath, this is perhaps not altogether to be wondered at.

At the time of this tale the pews, as was the fashion in kirks until quite recent times, were like large boxes without lids. Those inside could see the minister, who occupied a tall pulpit; but only when standing could they see the heads of their fellow-worshippers, or over the dividing partition which enclosed them.

There were seven seats in Mrs Irvine's pew, but, on this occasion, eight sitters. Next to the door was a worthy lawyer, who had slept through every sermon in that particular seat for the last quarter of a century. He was a man of methodical habits. He rose early every day from Monday to Saturday, and kept perfectly sober from the morning of the former day until about six o'clock on the evening of the latter. Sometime between that hour and midnight, however, he had invariably to be helped home, where he generally snored off his over-plentiful potations, without removing any more of his clothing than his hat. Awakening on the Sabbath he changed his clothes to those dedicated to Sunday and funeral use only, and, as he termed it, "cleaned" himself.

Cleanliness was not one of those things to which our Scottish forefathers dedicated either much time or attention. To shave and to have a good wash once a week was, to them, ample ablutions: a rub with a wet towel, serving well enough at other times.

So it was with Mistress Irvine's church pew neighbour; and the air, being sultry and stagnant within the confines of the "box," was by no means improved in condition by the distinct aroma of yesterday's rum which was exhaled from the mouth of the sleeping representative of the law.

Both the ladies, with whom we are acquainted, perspired freely, and felt most uncomfortable; even the standing up to pray, as was then the custom, having scarcely afforded any atmospheric relief.

The minister had at last concluded his final head of discourse, and his "finally and lastly" were merely memories, when the precentor rose up in his lower pulpit, and slowly read the banns.

He was just concluding "and this for the first, second, and third time," when all heads were turned in the direction of Mistress Irvine's pew, where a stout matron, with extremely warm-looking face, was standing up and crying at the pitch of her voice—

" I forbid the banns! I forbid the banns!"

The lawyer awakened with a start: Mrs Irvine was exerting all her power to pull her niece to her seat again, and some of the congregation had even mounted on to their seats in order to get a better view of what was going forward, when the stentorian tones of the minister were heard summoning "that woman" to meet him in the vestry at the conclusion of the divine worship.

During the short part of the service which remained, the lawyer took good care to enter into conversation with our two lady friends, and was not long in getting particulars from them; cunningly suggesting that, a lawyer would be as well to accompany them, to watch over their interests like.

The congregation dispersed at length; and then the minister's man ushered the trio into the sanctum which, in those days, was held in deep reverence, not unmixed with fear, by the majority of the members of kirk congregations.

The whole story was at length told, in spite of the lawyer's fussy interruptions, which greatly hindered the recital. It was a curious tale that the minister heard, and between the younger woman insisting that Scott it was who had carried off her daughter in the first place, while the elder blamed it on M'Innes, and the generally contradictory accounts he got, the reverend gentleman found he could make very little of the matter.

He said, however, he would think about it, and would certainly see this Thomas Mason, whom Lucky Thomson declared must be everything that was bad; if, indeed, it was his own name at all.

When just about to dismiss the party, the door opened, and no other than Thomas Mason himself was shown in. Conway had been at the kirk, and had hurried away to tell his friend what had happened.

Mason lost no time in hurrying back with him. Entering the vestry he bowed to the company and asked, in a respectful manner, why the banns had been forbidden? The two ladies were both going to speak, but were immediately silenced by the minister, who demanded from Mason a full and truthful statement of all he had to do with the affair.

This was soon given, but as it differed from Mistress Irvine's statements altogether in many important particulars, that lady at length lost all control of herself; after a vain endeavour to accomplish her former intention of scratching Mason's face, she eventually had to be carried out into the outer lobby of the kirk, where, finding her screams made no impression on the massive stone walls, they very soon ceased. Wishing to get out as quickly as possible she tried the door, but found that the minister's man, " entirely by a mistake," as he afterwards said, had locked her in the gloomy place, from which she did not escape until the bells rang for afternoon service.

Lucky Thomson's objections to Mason were, of course, entirely founded on her rooted detestation of all gaugers; but, being a woman of quick wit, she very soon came to the conclusion that a gauger, as a son-in-law, would be a very much easier person to have business relations with, than if there was no such connection.

So she very soon listened to the minister's advice, which, being sure in his own mind of Mason's truthfulness, was that she should give her consent to the proposed marriage. At the same time she was much too cunning to let this resolve on her part appear. She still insisted on Kate coming home with her; and all the encouragement or hope she held out for the now well-nigh distracted lover was, " that nae doot some o' thae days, he micht be in her country-side, and he could look in, and she wad bear him nae ill will."

Mason thus had to fetch Kate to her that very evening, and having found a lodging for mother and daughter, he hastened away as quickly as possible, as the mother's face clearly showed that a storm was brewing of no ordinary intensity.

The following Sunday the minister of the High Kirk preached on the evil of telling lies; and although his remarks were exhaustive, he yet found time to touch on the even greater sin of gaiety in any form, but more especially in the shape of concert-going and play-acting.

Mistress Irvine's face was scarlet beyond the possibilities even of rouge, and the fact that her neighbour the lawyer did not sleep at all, but looked ever and anon at her, did not tend to make her feel more at ease with herself, or at peace with all mankind.

On the same day Mason could have been found at Tranent, where he very soon learnt that Lucky Thomson full well knew the more than ordinary strong hold she had over him. But he bided his time, and, at last, the mother found that his continual visits were a serious interruption both to her contraband and her regular trade; for her customers being largely smugglers, they did not approve of a house where their conversation had so often to be reserved and circumspect. Besides, there was the danger at any time, of some of them unthinkingly saying something that would commit them all.

One evening, accordingly, she was visited by a deputation, who told her very plainly, that if she didn't get rid of this objectionable visitor altogether and at once, by letting him marry Kate, they would transfer their custom to Biddy's down in the " Pans."

So it was in the process of time brought about that Thomas Mason, of His Majesty's Customs, married Kate, only daughter of Lucky Thomson, dealer in contraband and other goods.

CHAPTER XIV.

IF further evidence to that already gathered were wanted to establish the fact that Shakespere either wrote the tragedy of "Macbeth" while actually resident in Scotland, or else produced it while the recollections of a recent trip to that northern portion of the kingdom were still fresh in his memory, it could be afforded in his terrifically graphic picture of the three witches—

"How now, you filthy, black, and midnight hags?"

This, and a score of other passages, show that their writer either had ocular evidence of the existence of such extraordinary creatures, or had listened to those to whom their appearance was familiar. There were witches, indeed, in England, but they were of a different species. There was no more comparison between one of the southern breed and her sister across the Tweed, than between the pock-puddin' Englishman and the gaunt and grisly warrior of the north, or, indeed, the roast beef of the one country and the pease brose of the other.

For aught that the writer knows to the contrary, the witches of old England might have been as deeply leagued with his Satanic Majesty as those of the north, but the uncanny and weird appearance of the latter had no counterpart in the former. Not only in the pages of Shakespere, but of Sir Walter Scott, and other writers, we have faithful descriptions of this class of woman.

They were to be found in Scotland even so late as the end of last century, and were so unearthly and fiendish in appearance and nature, that we really scarcely can wonder at the more than Draconian measures that were resorted to for their punishment and suppression.

Meg Merrilees, at times, possessed a queen-like and generous nature that few of her sisterhood could pretend to; and the crone who has already been introduced into this tale, although having no regal attributes about her, was, like her more famous sister in fiction, closely allied with the smuggling profession. Jen Dodds, in fact, for such was the beldam's name, although

in many respects but little better than half-
witted, was sufficiently sharp and cunning in
certain matters, to make her valuable as a spy,
both on Custom House officers and on the minor
although more active members among the fraternity of smugglers. She was immensely useful to those who were deeply interested in the
trade, and was well paid by them to look after
their interests. Her habit was to lie in wait
and watch, never showing herself save in the
dramatic and mysterious manner already recounted. She had often been able to advise the
head merchants of the trade in Edinburgh and
Jedburgh of important pieces of information
regarding those in their employ; and many a
consignment of contraband goods had been
saved by the timely warning she had been able
to give of the presence of officers on the lookout.

Unknown to Scott, and indeed to Helen Kenway or any of the rest, she had listened outside
the Cleekim Inn, on the evening with which our
tale opens, and heard, without any difficulty, the
tone of conversation in which the men were in-
dulging regarding the rising. What she had
endeavoured to do was to act upon their super-

M

stitious natures, and, if possible, dissuade them from leaving their illegal occupation. The manner in which she acted we have already seen, and it is only likely, had it not been for Scott's resolution and promptitude, she would have succeeded. That Scott was living in Edinburgh, she had discovered before any one else. She had the best chance, it is true, for she was seldom off the streets, lurking in some corner or another; and she was just planning how she could contrive to frighten or persuade him back into the clutches of his former masters, when chance flung him in her way in the manner we have seen.

As to her prophetic forebodings of evil, they were part of what we may term her other self, and will no more bear analysis than any other incidents of a mysterious or uncanny nature.

In her constant wanderings, she picked up many pieces of information, and, as we have seen, such knowledge she could frequently use in an extremely impressive and awe-inspiring manner. As for her ambiguously worded prophecies, being frequently founded on knowledge previously gained, they more often turned out true than might have been supposed. She was, heart and soul, a defier of all laws, human and divine; but, although knowing no sense of honesty or truth, she had never behaved in anything but an honourable manner to her employers. Their interests were hers, and it mattered not who suffered, their behests were obeyed, if within her power. Hers was a pure case of "honour among thieves," which has rightly been defined to extend only so far as mutual interests exist.

She left Scott, as we have seen, as suddenly and as mysteriously as she had encountered him; hurrying to certain of her superiors, to whom she made known her success in getting hold of Scott, and received her reward for bringing that worthy once more into the fold of the smuggling fraternity.

The crowd that had followed Scott was both baffled and mystified by that individual's sudden disappearance. All the force they could exert failed to open the door that had been slammed almost in their faces; but bent upon their prey, some of the crowd were proceeding in quest of a likely battering-ram, when there appeared on the scene a little, decrepit, old man, much bent with age, and carrying a bunch of keys, whose size and weight proclaimed, without donbt, they were of an ecclesiastical nature.

A stout beam had just been secured, and was about to be set in motion to break in the door; when, pushing his way through the throng, the key-bearer called out, in a high, squeaky voice—

"Get oot there, an' leave alane! G' wa wi' ye an' leave the door alane! Are ye wantin' the deid bodies that's in there? for there's nae-thing else tae find, I'm tellin' ye."

A dozen voices, in chorus, began telling him how a runaway thief and murderer had escaped them through that very door, and that they must get in to secure him.

This made no impression on the old man, who sarcastically remarked—"Ay An' hoo did he win in; maybe ye'll tell me. Was't through the key-hole?"

"No!" roared one of the roughest of the crowd. "The door was open, an' he just plumpit in, an' slammed it in oor faces. Come on, cal-lants, an' burst it in!"

"Stop, stop, my braw lads!" calmly rejoined the possessor of the keys. "No jist in sic a hurry. Ye say that there's a man gane in there.

Weel, it's ma thocht ye're jist speakin' a parcel
o' havers. Ye needna fash wi' that muckle
thing. Here's the key o' the door, an' I'll open
it tae ye fast enough, if there's ane o' ye bauld
enough tae walk in amang the human banes and
deid corpses that's lyin' intilt."

This last announcement checked in a marked
degree the eagerness of the crowd for explora-
tion, but one of the number, who was unaware
that the old man was sexton, as well as
minister's man in Greyfriars close by, demanded
his authority for the statement. This only
elicited a query as to whether there was " ony
mair wad like tae see for theirsels what was
intil the vault ? "

Mark Turnbull—for such was the sexton's
name—had held his post well-nigh forty years,
and in his own estimation was much the most
important personage, not only in the Greyfriars
Kirk, but in the whole Kirk of Scotland. The
minister of his own particular kirk he patron-
ised in a most condescending manner, and, as
for the elders and deacons, he thought it beneath
his dignity to acknowledge their greetings if they
happened to wish him a good day. A deputation had been sent from the synod not long

before these events, to suggest to Mark that, in view of his advancing years, he should retire upon a pension.

"Ay," said he, in reply to the spokesman of the party, "I mind sin syne, it may be saxteen year, there was four o' them cam tae me wi' the same story, that I was ower auld for the wark, but, ma certes, I've happit three o' them since then."

Mark had very strong reasons for not wishing to be put on his retiring allowance, for, as a matter of fact, he was deeply interested in the contraband business, and the very vault about which the discussion was going on, and which communicated also with the kirkyard, was a favourite place of storage for all kinds of merchandise that had not paid the king's duty. It was splendidly adapted for such a use, and had any one thought of lifting the lids of some of the coffins, they would certainly have been surprised at their contents—spirits instead of bodies would have been found inside.

Mark had himself seen the old hag enter the vault with Scott, and knew well that they would both escape by the secret door already mentioned. He didn't want, however, a crowd of prying eyes to be let loose inside, as some of them might light upon something else than bones, in which case his own ruin would result as a matter of course.

He very shrewdly concluded in his own mind that it would not be difficult to "pile on the agony," so to speak, and make superstition do what force or argument could not achieve; so, as there was no response to his query as to any-one else wanting to explore the vault, he inserted and slowly turned the key of the great lock, and, holding the door half-open, beckoned to the youth who had alone demanded his authority for stating that bones alone lay within.

"Gang on, ma man," shouted one and another in the crowd, "gang in an' see for yersel; I'm thinkin' Mark should ken best onyway."

With these and similar remarks the youth was shoved towards the door, into which he was finally impelled by an application of the toe of Mark's boot, a rude sort of practical joke that exactly suited the humorous capacity of the crowd, and the grin of laughter that appeared on their countenances was immediately changed to a shout of laughter when Mark nimbly pulled to the door, turned the key, and marched off in

the direction of the very public-house in which
Scott was sitting in hiding. Some half-dozen
or more, who were known to Mark, entered
along with the sexton while the remainder of
the crowd dispersed.

An hour afterwards the key was again inserted, and the prisoner, in a state of fear
amounting almost to madness, was liberated, and
he was glad to flee from the scene under a perfect
storm of ridicule from Mark and his now somewhat inebriated cronies.

CHAPTER XV.

IT is useless for the purposes of this story to follow the fortunes, or we should perhaps say misfortunes, of Will. Scott, during the seven or eight months following his escape from Edinburgh.

Without any desire on his part—in fact, much against his will—he had drifted back into his old course of life, without apparently any possibility of freeing himself from its clutches. His recent short experience of life was a · living example of the truth of the proverb, "As you make your bed, so must you lie on it." The same truth is nowadays being preached from the house-tops by scientists as quite a discovery in philosophy; but most *good* truths are old, and whether they come to us in their homely guise or clothed in scientific habiliments it makes little difference, so long as we understand them, and do our best to act up to the good advice they convey.

Scott now smuggled in the west country: a region quite new to him, and which did not come under the superintendence of his particular foe, Mason. It is not surprising, therefore, that he escaped detection, and did a splendid trade, more especially as the country was in a very disturbed state, and the gaugers not by any means up to their work.

The summer of 1746 passed, and with it, as we all know, the hopes of the Stuarts for ever. The autumn came, and once again the woods of Teviotdale were dyed in ruddy hues. The river was mightily swollen, for the storm had lasted many days, and the wind roared among the trees as they swayed to and fro.

It was exactly one year from the day that Will. Scott last had entered the Cleekim Inn. As the day wore on, from morning to afternoon, Helen Kenway went to the door and looked long and anxiously, first to the north, then to the west, then to the east, and lastly, by traversing the distance to the corner of the house, to the south, in which direction the pines bent with the wind so as almost to hide the road from view. But nobody was in sight, and Helen Kenway returning to the door, and in the manner

in which it was usual for her to make announce-
ments of the sort to her elder companion, said,
" There's nane in sicht, so we'll just spile a gude
denner gin we cook it."

" Gud a mercy, but that wud be awfu'!"

" Weel, weel, Marget, may be we'd better;
syne they dae come, there wad be an awfu' kick
up if they didna find their kail het, sae pit it
on !"

As the day wore on the storm abated, and all
the forces of nature seemed to have gone to rest.
The sun shone out in fullest glory, and the
birds whistled gaily once more to welcome its
bright rays. Afternoon arrived, and suddenly
four or five horsemen reined up at the door, and
jumping down they made fast their horses
and bustled noisily into the inn. Helen
Kenway knew but one of them; it was Will.
Scott.

" An ye hae come back tae pay me ma
reckonin', ma bonnie man ? "

" Ay, that hae I ; an' what aboot the denner ? "

" Oh, it's a' ready, het an' reekin ; but whae
are yer freends ? "

" New freends, ma lassie—the auld anes are
a' gane ! "

"Gud a mercy, but that's awfu'," put in Marget from a respectful distance.

"Ay, it is," replied Scott, "but tae hell wi' care; bring oot the drink an' let's mak merry, ma lads, a short life an' a merry ane. I've seen some queer ups and douns, and nane mair sae than this last twalmonth's syne." And so the talk continued; and as the feast continued the conversation got higher and the drink flowed faster, until by the time when the moon rose without, to shed its silver rays upon a scene of peace, and what might have been goodwill to all men, within there was nothing but swearing and cursing, and that excess in everything, that to some people gives the lie to the manifest good that exists in the initial design of all things earthly.

The moon gave light to guide and cheer the path of two individuals that night, both of whom were journeying towards the Cleekim Inn. The one was on horseback, the other on foot; the former was a tall man wrapped in a great cloak, the latter, a miserable looking old hag clothed in rags, and supporting herself with a rude staff. She had evidently walked far, and was much fatigued. To judge, however, by certain mut-

terings that escaped her lips from time to
time, she possessed some strong motive for con-
tinuing her journey with all the speed possible. When within a mile of the inn, the
sound of horses' hoofs making up on her
caught her ear. Stopping for an instant and
listening intently with her head to the ground,
she muttered, "Am I ower late, after a'?" and,
jumping to her feet again, hurried on more
quickly than before. At intervals she might
have been heard muttering such sentences as
the following—"Can I no stop him?" "Will
he be alane?" "Will I no be in time?"—all
evincing a state of great mental excitement in
connection with the approach of the horseman.
A few more minutes must have allowed the
rider to overtake the footsore and tired pedes-
trian, when he seemed to slacken his pace, a fact
instantly remarked by the crone, who, now that
some chance of keeping in front presented itself to
her, seemed stimulated to even greater exertions.
The inn, with its lights brightly shining through
the small windows, was now in sight, and the
horseman was still some distance behind; so
muttering something unintelligible, she made
an ungainly dash towards her destination. A

momentary peep through the window seemed to satisfy her that she had reached the object of her forced march, and without pausing she entered the inn and stood in front of Scott and his companions, now all far gone in liquor. Breathless, from the speed at which she had travelled, for a moment she could do no more than raise her skinny hand and point with one long bony finger at Scott. She stood opposite a roaring fire of pine logs, the red glow from which shone full upon her weird form, a sight calculated to at least astonish, if not to frighten even men of unsuperstitious minds, and in this case, where those who beheld her were both superstitious and tipsy, the effect she produced was startling. Jumping from their seats, in their hurry the men upset the rude table upon which stood their drink, but without pausing, they made for the door with one intent. To win the point of exit they had to pass the hag, who, between her gasps for breath, both implored and ordered them to remain where they were. She might as well have spoken to the fallen table and bid it rise. What little capacity for reflection the creatures did possess, was now drowned in strong drink, and, sheeplike, a move having been made, nothing would stay them. In the midst of the hurry-scurry Scott, who had risen, but had not moved from his place, cried—

"So ye are there again, ye hag o' hell; I mind yer words weel. Ane o' us maun dee, an' it's you that wull. Tak that;" saying which, he raised a pistol and fired. As he did so, his hand was knocked up from behind by Helen Kenway, and the ball entered the rough beams of the ceiling.

"What did ye dae that for, ye meddlin' quean?" roared Scott, aiming a blow with the butt end of his weapon at the landlady's head, but she dodged it neatly, and said with perfect composure, "There's tae be nae bluid shed in ma house; gae wa ootside an' blaw aff yer guns, an' dinna come in here wi' them. Dae ye no see it's only an auld witch; what wad ye fire on the likes o' her for?" Turning to the hag, she said—

"What dae ye want in here, ma wumman? I'll gie ye a drink, an' then be gane."

"It's him I want. Flee, Wull Scott," shrieked the woman, now fairly supplied with breath; "flee, man, the gauger's here, an' it's for you he's come."

" Bah," replied the smuggler, " let him come. Lucky, here's yer reckonin'; dae ye mind I'm owin' ye for last time; here's twa croons. Is't eneuch ? "

" Eneuch, man ? ma certes, no; was there no ten o' ye here this day twalmonth, an' dae ye think twa croons 'll pay for them a'."

" I'll pay for nae man but mysel', sae be satisfeed."

" Ye'll pay me ma reckonin' in full, an' for yer freends, this nicht; and look what they've broken. Pay me, ma man, or it'll be the worse for ye."

" Dinna threat me, woman; as for the scaith, yon hag's to blame."

" Ay, ay, I'll pay," screeched the hag, " but get ye gane, Wull Scott. Eh, man ! wull ye no gang in time ? "

Long ere this the sound of the horses' hoofs, belonging to the frightened smugglers, had died away in the distance. A dead silence fell for a moment on the scene, which so recently had been all turmoil. Scott still stood with the pistol clubbed in his hand, regarding with fixed eye the uncouth being in front of him, who, to enforce her pleading, had dropped on her knees. Helen stood looking at the smuggler with a face full of hate, and, when in that position, all three were startled by the entrance of a fourth. It was Marget who rushed in, and in what might be called a stage whisper, said—

"Gud a mercy, there's a man at the ootside, what are we tae dae?"

"Only ane?" queried Scott.

"Ay, ay; but dinna, dinna, I've steeked the door."

This appeal was made to Scott, who had stepped towards the entranee with the evident intention of going outside. The hag also addressed him, and even laid hold of his coat in her excitement.

"Na, na, ye'll be safer here, bide an' ye're safe."

But Scott was in no mood to accede to any request or demand, and throwing off the grip of the one, and thrusting the other from his path, he strode to the door, which he opened and stepped out. Brighter than the moonlight, a long shaft of light from the inn room window lay like a golden path across the roadway, getting broader but fainter the further it stretched away from the building. Just beside it, and partly lit by this luminous streak, stood Thomas Mason.

"What dae ye want?" growled Scott.

"You," replied Mason, as he advanced slowly, fixing his eye steadily the while on the other.

Scott's right hand still grasped the empty pistol. Recollecting the fact, he flung it to the ground with a curse, and gripped the butt of another in his belt, from which he never drew it forth. Another pistol than his had sent forth its messenger of Death, and the body of the smuggler fell to the earth with a dull thud.·

There was an unearthly shriek from a woman within the door. The hag rushed forth and dragged Mason into the light that streamed from the window. So sudden, so unexpected was the onslaught, that the officer did not raise a finger until he stood with the glare full upon his face. Then he would have thrown the woman from him, but her words rooted him to the spot, and made his blood almost to freeze in his veins.

"Thomas Mason, ye hae killed the faither o' yer ain flesh an' bluid, and the grandfaither o' them that's tae come."

"Speak, woman, what do ye mean?" he demanded.

"What dae I mean? I mean that Katie Tamson was that man's dochter; she's yer wife, and she'll be the mither o' his grandchildren."

They came in the morning and dug a grave, where the four roads met; and when the earth had been shovelled over the clay that lately had been the smuggler Will. Scott, the old crone hung around the spot, and chanted to herself in grumbling tone—

> "He has keepit his tryste
> And gane to hell;
> Nae buik nor priest had he,
> Nor passing bell."

FINIS.

Printed by T. and A. Constable, Printers to Her Majesty
at the Edinburgh University Press

www.ingramcontent.com/pod-product-compliance
Lightning Source LLC
Chambersburg PA
CBHW030538040726
47497CB00008B/2503